I0763341

ARK OF THE COVENANT

Ark of the Covenant

ISBN: 978-0-9988777-3-0 (hardback)
978-0-9988777-4-7 (paperback)
978-0-9988777-5-4 (ebook)

Printed in the United States of America

ARK OF THE COVENANT

Raid on the Church of Our Lady Mary of Zion

Gary J. Rose

DEDICATION

I am fortunate as a writer to be surrounded by a great support group of relatives, friends, and co-workers who unknowingly, in each of their various ways, help me through those long months needed to complete a novel. I want to thank my two cousins, Dr. Fred Vallier and Dr. Jane Vallier for their participation in bringing this book to publication.

Special thanks to Debbie Lum for volunteering hours needed to proof-read my final manuscript and making valuable suggestions.

To R'tor John Maghuyop, thank you for another great formatting and cover design.

Finally, to my readers, I sincerely believe in my quote, "When you stop dreaming or using your imagination, you are starting to die. I hope that this book will inspire you to dream and use your imagination.

—The Author

The books of Gary J. Rose

Towards the Integration of Police Psychology Techniques to Combat Juvenile Delinquency in K-12 Classroom

Hitting Rock Bottom

A NOTE TO READERS

Biblical scholars, and indeed members of the public, in other words, most of the world, started to wonder, after the release of the hit movie, "Raiders of the Lost Ark," where the actual Ark of the Covenant is presently located, or at least, what happened to it.

Today, speculations and theories continue, and the number of possibilities are numerous, including claims of actual possession of the Ark.

According to the Old Testament, the Ark was kept in the Temple of Solomon in Jerusalem for centuries, but after that city was conquered by the Babylonians in the 6th century BC, its exact location became unclear (Isaiah 37:14-16

There are suggestions that the Ark is hidden somewhere on Mount Nebo near the Jordan River, somewhere on the East Bank. Some believe it was hidden in a cave or buried, and lost forever. Other scholars believe that the prophet Jeremiah ordered that the tent and the Ark of the Covenant be placed in a cave on the mountain where Moses received the Ten Commandments.

And Jeremiah came and found a cave, and he brought there the tent and the ark and the altar of incense, and he sealed up the entrance. Some of those who followed him came up to mark the way, but could not find it." When Jeremiah learned of it, he rebuked them and declared: "The place shall be unknown until God gathers his people together again and shows his mercy. And then the Lord will disclose these things, and the glory of the Lord and the cloud will appear, as they were shown in the case of Moses, and as Solomon asked that the place should be specially consecrated." And the Lord will disclose these things, and the glory of the Lord and the cloud will appear, as they were shown in the case of Moses, and as Soloman asked that the place should be specially consecrated."Jeremiah 3:16 (The Ark of the Covenant of the LORD)

And when you have multiplied and increased in the land, in those days, says the LORD, they shall no more say, "The ark of the covenant of the LORD." It shall not come to mind, or be remembered, or missed; it shall not be made again.

Enter the Ethiopians, who claim that they in fact, possess the Ark, and that it was brought to Ethiopia by King Menelik approximately 3,000 years ago. They said that, as quoted in the Bible, a child of King Solomon and the Queen of Sheba brought the Ark to their country just prior to the fall of Temple of Solomon. The story is told in the *Kebra Negast* (Glory of the Kings), Ethiopia›s chronicle of its royal line:

the Queen of Sheba, one of its first rulers, traveled to Jerusalem to partake of King Solomon's wisdom. On her way home, she bore Solomon's son, Menelik. Later Menelik went to visit his father, and on his return journey was accompanied by the firstborn sons of some Israelite nobles—who, unbeknown to Menelik, stole the Ark and carried it with them to Ethiopia. When Menelik learned of the theft, he reasoned that since the Ark's frightful powers hadn't destroyed his retinue, it must be God's will that it remain with him. The Ethiopians claim that for many years their country, Ethiopia, has cared for the Ark.

Under their control, the Ark has been moved many times for security reasons and now resides in Aksum, in the Tigray Province in the Chapel of the Tablet. The Chapel itself is a very curiously shaped building, surrounded by spiked wrought iron sections of fencing, and strategically placed between two churches, one being old and one being new. All part of what is named, Church of St. Mary of Zion.

The Chapel of the Tablet and the newer of the two St. Mary of Zion churches were built in the 1960s. Once completed, the Ark of the Covenant was moved into its new location and have been there ever since according the Orthodox church authorities.

A monk, known as the "guardian," is entrusted with the preservation and care of the Ark. Even the head of Ethiopian church is forbidden from seeing the Ark. The guardian of the Ark is the only person on earth who has the peerless honor to view it. The guardian's duties remain until death falls upon him. He cannot leave the Chapel of the Tablets: in fact, it is forbidden by the Ethiopian Orthodox Church, except for walking around the ground surrounding the building enclosed by the spiked wrought iron fencing. While on his deathbed, he is to name his successor. If he dies before doing so, the church, similar to the selection of a new Roman Catholic pope, will make the selection. Which brings us to the question of how the Vatican (Roman Catholic Church) feels about the location of the Ark of the Covenant. In the New Testament, the Ark is mentioned in the Letter to the Hebrews and the Revelation of St. John. Hebrews 9: states that the Ark contained "the golden pot that had manna, and Aaron's rod that budded, and the tablets of the covenant." Revelation 11:19 says the prophet saw God's temple in heaven opened, "and the Ark of his Covenant was seen within his temple."

Roman Catholic writers connect this verse with the Woman of the Apocalypse in Revelation 12:1, which immediately follows, and say that the Blessed Virgin Mary is the «Ark of the New Covenant.» Carrying the savior of mankind within her, she herself became the Holy of Holies. This is the interpretation given in the third century by Gregory Thaumaturgus, and in the fourth century by Saint Ambrose, Saint Ephraem of Syria and Saint Augustine. The Catholic Church teaches this in the Catechism of the Catholic Church:

«Mary, in whom the Lord himself has just made his dwelling, is the daughter of Zion in person, the Ark of the Covenant, the place where the glory of the Lord dwells. She is 'the dwelling of God . . . with men».

In the Gospel of Luke, the author's accounts of the Annunciation and Visitation are constructed using eight points of literary parallelism to compare Mary to the Ark.

It is believed by Roman Catholics, that Athanasius, the bishop of Alexandria, wrote about the connections between the Ark and the Virgin Mary: "O noble Virgin, truly you are greater than any other greatness. For who is your equal in greatness, O dwelling place of God the Word? To whom among all creatures shall I compare you, O Virgin? You are greater than them all O (Ark of the) Covenant, clothed with purity instead of gold! You are the Ark in which is found the golden vessel containing the true manna, that is, the flesh in which Divinity resides" (*Homily of the Papyrus of Turin*). However, some question the authenticity of this work and suggest it is an example of the writing of yet another Pseudo-Athanasius.

With no definitive answers as to what happened or the present-day location of the physical Ark of the Covenant, one can only speculate as to its present day location.

"When you stop dreaming or using your imagination, you start to die."

—Gary Rose

CHAPTER 1

November 11, 2001, a combined joint Special Operations Task Force-South, otherwise known as Task Force S-Bar, was gearing up for their next mission. Task Force S-Bar had already carried out several Special Reconnaissance and Direct Action missions in the South of Afghanistan starting in October 2001. Of course, since all their missions were classified as Black Ops, the public would never learn of their tasks until well after the Gulf War ended and maybe never.

Task Force S-Bar consisted of Navy SEALS, U.S. Army Special Forces, Special Warfare Combatant-craft Crewman, a USAF Combat Controller, and Special Forces Units from Canada, Norway, New Zealand, Australia, Germany, Denmark and Turkey.

Sergeant Frank Silva was squad leader of a specialized unit of Army Rangers attached to Task Force S-Bar. A veteran of the Panama operation, his team, consisting of four Ranger specialists, was highly regarded, even by their biggest foe, the SEALS. He and his team, even earned a nickname from the SEALS, who called them the *Banshees.*

With all the notoriety of the Navy SEALS as the nation's most highly trained special forces units, even over the famed Green Berets and Delta Force, there was more than just rivalry between the Banshees and the SEALS. Known for their unorthodox methods and trail of death that remained as the only evidence of their missions, the SEALS felt that the Banshees were a bunch of undisciplined thugs, but they still admired them for always completing their missions.

They had been the subject of numerous inquiries about their viciousness and possible "war crimes," yet they always seemed to be able to justify their actions. Still, the SEALS and other combat troops questioned their methods but not their ability. None of these other units would ever object upon learning that the Banshees had been assigned as backup to their missions.

At first, Frank and his team took offense to the term given to their squad, since they knew that the word *Banshee,* referred to a wailing women in Irish folklore, whose wailing warns of an impending death. But, after a while, they liked this reference of the warning of impending death, and decided that Irish folklore needed to be updated with a male Banshee addition; and thus, their team relished in being referred to simply as the Banshees.

Frank's team lost their lieutenant in a fire-fight or at least it was staged to look like he was killed by the enemy. They had decided to eliminate their lieutenant after he caught them stealing valuables from a dead terrorist. Using the weapon of the terrorist, Frank shot him in the back, killing him instantly. They shared no remorse for their action – instead felt that he would receive a damn medal and his wife back home would receive his death benefits. Since the team operated just as efficiently or better with Frank, no immediate plans were made to replace him by HQ.

Frank had been summoned to headquarters for briefing on a new mission to be executed by his team this evening. Colonel Thompson was late to the briefing room, but once he arrived, it was all business. A large operations map was pinned to the cork board covered by a large sheet of plastic with several different colored arrows, indicating prior, present, or future operations.

Frank's squad had a search and destroy mission. He was told that they were to drop behind enemy lines and destroy a Tomahawk cruise missile which had crashed in the desert before reaching its target.

Shit, Frank thought, this will be a hard sell once again to his men. But, this was the price that had to be paid when the President forms a coalition of forces for friendly nations to take on Iraq. He recalled reading somewhere, that General Eisenhower had to do the same thing during World War II, which really pissed off some of his generals, especially Old Blood and Guts, General Patton.

But, the Banshees were an elite squad, and this really seemed to be a waste of their talent. It would do no good to plead for a different assignment and since his squad just got cleared for alleged military injustice, Frank just sucked it up. He and his team knew that this was becoming a new "politically correct" Armed Forces with damn military and civilian attorneys second guessing every move they made in the field. He remembers some of the stupid questions he and his team were asked after their last mission in which they killed seven hostiles, "Did the victim fire first?" "Victim?" he was the enemy pointing a AK-47 directly at me. "No, he did not fire first. I got him before he got me." Jesus, what a stupid question!

Unfortunately, these post-mission interviews were becoming interrogations, and Special Forces units were not exempt. Frank's team was very experienced in how to stage an engagement after the fight, so that anyone entering the scene to Monday morning quarterback would have to conclude that justified actions were taken.

Frank went back to his unit, and after getting everyone together, explained their mission.

"Shit, Frank, why doesn't HQ just drop a bunch of fuckin lawyers over there and have them negotiate with the camel jockeys to get their missile back?" asked Ed. "No, we have to locate the dud, risk getting our asses shot off, and then, God forbid, we blow away a mother-fucker who tries to blow us away; we then have to defend our actions."

"Any other bitching gentlemen?" Frank asked.

Frank then issued each of them a pack. "What is this?" Ruben asked.

"This is your nuclear, biological, contamination suit." Frank replied. "Since Saddam is getting his ass kicked, Intel feels that he may become more desperate and could start using biologicals on us. Remember, that prick used them on his own people."

"Fuck Intel," Ruben said. "Who the hell expects us to wear this walking condom and do our job? "Frank, unless you order me to wear it, it can stay right here in its nice little pouch so it will not get dirty."

"It is up to each of you. For me, I don't want to walk around as a condom either," Frank said. "Ok, get ready to move out in fifteen minutes."

The Banhsees helocasted off the Kuwaiti coast before coming ashore where they met up with Kuwaiti agents who drove them to the crash site. With the help of these agents, it was a piece of cake in locating the item.

Joe and Jessie attached the C-4 explosives to the dud, while Frank and Ruben provided cover and started back to a safe location for detonation. They then heard what sounded like an approaching convoy. They took cover and observed. It was a Republican Guard unit, escorting a SCUD missile carrier. This was a huge concern by the U.S. government going into the war. Iraq had purchased God knows how many SCUDs from Russia and had been launching them from various sites into Israel.

Frank recalled at one of his HQ briefings that if Israel decided to leave their border and invade other Arab lands in retaliation for SCUD attacks, this could cause some major problems with the alliance which would start to collapse. This is what Saddam predicted and hoped for in advance of the war.

SCUDs were a lot harder to locate and destroy since they were mobile. Stationary targets were easily eliminated by the coalition's air power and were destroyed almost immediately at the beginning of the conflict.

All told, there were eight Republican Guardsmen. Frank motioned to Jessie, Joe, Ed, and Ruben, which two guardsmen, were their targets. Frank would pick his targets at random, making sure that anyone hit by his team would be dead for sure. There would be no chance for surrender. The Banshees do not take prisoners. This was a big reason for their fame with the other Special Forces units.

It was over in less than a minute. Eight Republican Guardsmen lay dead where they once stood. So much for Saddam's elite unit.

Joe and Jessie, attached addional C-4 on the SCUD. Seeking cover, they destroyed the Tomahawk and SCUD, before returning to the sea for pickup by helicopter.

Frank's team thought the whole mission, even though they took out a SCUD battery, was a waste of their talent. Although they were trained for these missions, their expertise was political assassination or destroying high worth targets, not to blow up a dud missile and SCUD battery in the fucking desert.

As soon as the team returned to base camp, Frank was again requested to come to HQ. Frank hoped, for the sake of the morale of the Banshees, that they would receive a much more "rewarding" mission. Frank was not let down.

Whatever this next operation was, it was big. This was the first time that Frank, attending a meeting in HQ with other Special Forces units, found the room packed. Colonel Thompson entered the room, but before everyone could stand, he ordered them to be seated.

"Men, tonight, each of your units will be carrying out different missions. We will be hitting Saddam's troops in multiple locations. Some of these missions will be to disrupt the enemy, some will be search and destroy, and some will be to snatch and grab key high ranking Iraq officers.

While the colonel was speaking, his aides handed out mission folders to each Special Forces unit. Frank was given a folder that, when opened, got his juices following. Finally, a mission worthy of the Banshees. After completing his briefing, Frank returned to his squad and had them meet in his room. Entering the room were Ed, Joe, Ruben and finally, Jessie. Frank had been with these four specialists since Panama, and he felt that he could never have been assigned a better group to carry out the missions they were normally assigned. Tonight's assignment would be no different.

"This, gentlemen, is General Kamel Sajid of the Iraqi Republican Guard," Frank said as he pointed to a picture laying on his bed.

"Looks like all the other camel jockeys to me, Sarge," said Jessie. Everyone except Frank laughed.

"Intel has it that this asshole will be in this shithole of a town in this three-story building tonight. He will have his normal body guard contingent of six Republican guards. Our mission, if you haven't guessed it already, is to snatch and grab, or kill him and any other assholes who want to stop us from completing our task. Any questions?" Frank asked. No one said anything.

"Ok, we will meet at the chopper pad at 0100 hours. The weather tonight is supposed to be thunderstorms, so we will use the thunder to cover our advance. We will fast rope down to the roof of this building once Intel informs us that he is there.

Joe and Ed, you two will be our sniper unit on the roof. Jessie, Ruben and I will hit the house. Delta Force and Rangers will be driving in from here to take our prisoners once we tell them the "package" is ready. Joe and Ed laughed with Joe saying, "sure."

Once we turnover the general, we will go back to the roof, and provide sniper coverage for Delta and the Rangers, as they load the package and return to base. We will then be picked up by a chopper and return home for a cold beer or two." Frank looked around for any questions, but got none. They all knew there would be no prisoners.

"See you at 0100 hours," Frank said, as his team of Banshees left his room.

CHAPTER 2

Wearing night vision equipment and headsets, Frank and the Banshees boarded the chopper at 0118 hours. It took only 25 minutes to enter the outreach of the town. Approaching in whisper mode, the chopper followed a signal coming from a transmitter thrown onto the roof by a Kuwaiti operative earlier in the evening. This made the location easy to spot from the air. The thunder was wicked but did not seem to cause the chopper flight crew any problems.

Frank had received a "go" command from HQ, indicating that General Sajid was in the building, supposedly verified by Intel on the ground. Frank motioned to his team with a thumb's up, that it was a go, and for them to activate their night-vision. Approaching the door of the chopper and grabbing the repelling rope, Frank was the first one out the door. This was one of the things that the Banshees admired the most about Frank; he never asked them to do anything he would not do first.

Jessie, Ed, Ruben and finally Joe, repelled down the ropes and regrouped with Frank on the roof. Using the roof access, Frank entered the building with his Sig Sauer P226 9mm with suppressor in his right hand. Jessie and Ruben entered next. Joe and Ed remained on the roof in opposite corners to scout the area from above with their U.S. Navy Mk-12

5.56 sniper rifles.

Meanwhile, after being notified that the Banshees had reached their location, the extraction team members, made up of Rangers and Delta Force, began their advance on the town in their Hummers to the location of the building.

Frank begin his descent from the third floor and heard male voices on the floor just below his location. He quickly raised his left hand made into a fist, commanding Jessie and Ruben to hold his position. Frank determined from the different voices, that there were at least eight individuals in the room. He reached quietly into his side pouch and pulled out a flash-bang grenade. Raising it up to show Jessie and Ruben what he had in his hand, they automatically knew what the game plan was.

Seeing Frank getting ready to throw the flash-bang grenade down the stairs, Jessie and Ruben prepared to quickly follow Frank into the second-floor room. Immediately after the flash-bang went off, there was a tremendous amount of automatic gunfire from AK-47s. The gunfire was sprayed by the people on the second floor out of desperation and several rounds hit their fellow soldiers.

Frank personally took out two Republican guards and Jessie took out three. Three appeared to take out each other while firing in panic. Ruben had not been able to get off a round due to his position in the rear. Frank motioned to Ruben to clear the first floor, which he did. Frank and Jessie began trying to identify if their target was among the dead. He was not. To verify, they both looked again. The general was not here as Intel predicted.

"Those motherfuckers! Whoever came up with the word "Army Intelligence" should be shot. Isn't that what they call an oxymoron?" asked Jessie.

Ruben returned from the first floor, indicating that it was clear. Frank and Jessie looked closer at the bodies to see which ones they had killed, and which ones killed each other. Finding which ones had AK-47 wounds, Frank told Reuben to give them double taps. No one, who might investigate later, can take away any kills by the Banshees. The myth and legend must continue, they all thought.

Frank called base command and said to cancel the extraction team since the target was not there. Operations acknowledged his transmission and ordered the extraction team to return to base.

Frank then called to the chopper pilot who had left the area after dropping off his team, ordering him to not return to the roof until notified, so that his team could gather any intelligence material from the building. The chopper pilot responded with a "roger that" as he kept the helicopter well out of range from the building.

Ordering Jessie and Ruben to start checking for anything worth gathering, Frank too, joined in the search. He looked at his watch and checked the time. In the center of the room was a table that had contained food items, now scattered around the floor. The floor was also covered with spent ammo, blood and human waste. Against one wall was a worn-out couch that now contained one Republican guardsman laying partly on his side.

What was not seen initially, resting to the side of the left arm rest of the couch, was a large briefcase. It was a lot larger than those carried by attorneys or professors. It appeared to be one of those that can be expanded when a person has a lot of documents or content. Frank motioned to Jessie to check it out, while he continued his search.

"Holy shit!" yelled Jessie, causing Frank and Ruben to grab their firearms and prepare for an engagement. Seeing no combatants, Frank and Ruben relaxed.

Frank asked him, "what is it?"

Saying nothing, Jessie poured the contents of the briefcase on the couch near the dead guardsman. Out spilled wrapped bundles of U.S. bills in hundred dollar denominations.

Frank walked over to Jessie as did Ruben. All three looked down at the cash. Each grabbed a bundle and began thumbing through them to get a rough count as to the value of each. Each bundle contained $10,000. What they found were fifty bundles equaling $500,000.

CHAPTER 3

Arriving back at base camp, Frank proceeded to HQ for debriefing.

"Sorry Frank," said Colonel Thompson. "We really thought the intel was reliable. At least your team eliminated a lot of bad guys and no one was hurt. Anything of value found inside the building?"

Frank looked at the colonel to see if he could read anything in his face or body language to suggest that he somehow knew about the stash they found. Seeing nothing to indicate that he said, "No sir. It seemed to me that perhaps we hit the house too soon. I mean, why would these guardsmen, all be meeting there? It was as if they were waiting for someone, maybe the general." Colonel Thompson replied, "That is what Intel is now thinking. Oh well, Frank, we can't win them all and there will be another day for the Banshees. Good job!"

With that, Frank knew that he was being dismissed.

Frank and the rest of the Banshees met up again, following his briefing with the colonel, in the base bar. Frank ordered a round for his team.

"What did the colonel say?" asked Ed.

"Typical bullshit. Sorry Frank, for you and your team. Good work. Sorry Intel was off. You killed a lot of bad guys. You'll get him next time. Same shit you hear in movies and television shows." Frank addressed the team.

"Any hint that he knows about the loot we found?" asked Joe.

"Not a word," Frank responded. "He did ask if we found anything of value? But, since I didn't think he was asking about you-know-what, I said no." Everyone either laughed or grinned.

"So now what?" asked Ruben.

Frank did not initially respond, but instead looked at his team, and then gathered around the bar to make sure his conversation could not be overheard. "Well guys, my suggestion is that we split the money equally among ourselves. I mean, think about it. No one will ever know on our side, who this money really belongs to. It could be opium money funneled to the Republican Guard for the war effort. It could belong to some fucking sheik who has so much money, he is not going to miss it. And then there is us (using his hand to encircle his team); soldiers, who, different from those asshole liberals back home, put our lives on the line during each tour of duty. Who better, deserves these spoils of war?" Frank waited for a response from anyone on his team.

Jessie did not disappoint, saying, "fuckin-a," I agree with Frank. If we somehow came up with a story to cover our asses and turn in the money, where would it go? Back to some asshole government agency to eventually line the pockets of those corrupt senators and congressman and women. I say, fuck them, let us keep the money and we will stimulate the economy when we get back to the states."

Frank saw that all agreed, so he told them to return to the bar after chow this evening and to bring something to carry their share. Each would receive $100,000.

That evening they met again. Frank, making sure no one in the bar was watching, handed the money to each of his team members, individually, under the table. He then told them to be patient and not spend any of the money on base, and to wait until they got states side. Even then he instructed them to be cautious on the use of the money, so as not to bring attention to them from friends, relatives and especially the IRS.

Chapter 4

April 2016 – Syrian Desert

As the winds started to die down, Abdel Fattah was finally able to focus on his paper target 30 feet down range. Armed with a Kalashnikov AK-47, he quickly demonstrated to his instructors, that he was competent in its use. Both using single burst and fully automatic, he was easily the best marksmen among the ISSI recruits.

After being recruited, he joined ISSI in early January after leaving his family, consisting of a wife and three children in Ethiopia. Raised a Christian, Fattah was introduced to Islam after the tragic death of both his mother and father in the first Gulf War. Unsatisfied with the dogma of the Christian faith, he stated that he found Islamic doctrine was much simpler and what he called rational. He was attracted to the equality of all believers and the fact that it lacks a priesthood – at least this is what he had ISSI believing for the cause of his conversion.

Like many Africans, he said that he believed that the Christian church was racist and felt discriminated against. Therefore, it was natural for him to reject the culture that would not have him. Related to his supposed new-found hatred of Christianity, he frequently made statements out loud in hopes of being heard, that Christians were the people doing these things and had to therefore be killed.

He told anyone who would listen to him that he also felt that the African society was disintegrating for lack of discipline, especially in their cities. Through its disciplined lifestyle, believers of Islam held out the promise of helping Muslims get their lives back in order again.

Islam is the only religion that offered him a conversion experience and the opportunity to get his life in order without needing to confess one's sin and need of salvation. In fact, Islam makes quite a point of denying these truths. He did not need salvation; all he needed was to follow the "guidance" of God's law, and he would make it to heaven. Fattah was sure that he had developed an excellent background of pro-ISSI propaganda, and that an ISSI recruit would notice him. He was correct, for shortly later, he was contacted by a recruiter who already knew much of Fattah's background and desire of allegiance to ISSI. Everything so far had worked as planned by him and his CIA handler.

Upon arriving at the terrorist training camp, Fattah continued the fraud of being radicalized and a committed jihadist. His enthusiasm and proven abilities were quickly noticed by those in command. He voiced that the tenets of Christianity had been replaced by a belief in Sharia Law and Sharia (law) for Islamists is the idea that they are duty-bound to implement and enforce medieval Islamic jurisprudence in their modern "Islamic state." He stated his devotion to Sharia Law and the need of enforcing women being veiled or suffer the consequences. Discriminating against women and non-Muslims and implementing penal codes such as amputations, floggings, beheadings and stoning of offenders to death, he decreed was now sacred to him and that it was a God-given duty that cannot be changed.

The order was given for the recruits to secure their weapons and run to the obstacle course. Before it was Fattah's turn to crawl through the pipes laying on the desert floor, one of his instructors called to him. Lightly brushing the desert sand from his clothing, Fattah immediately obeyed the command and approached his instructor.

"Come with me," was the next command. Fattah was motioned to a large tent located off from the main compound. He knew that drone attacks at other ISSI's training camps seem to target the center of their compounds and the command tent was constantly being relocated. This camp so far, praise Allah he thought many times, had not been the focus of any drone attacks.

CHAPTER 5

Entering the tent, Fattah saw sitting at the end of a large throw rug, was the camp commander, Abu Habib al-Otaibi. He was a legend among the recruits having escaped numerous target bombings and kidnappings by America and their allied forces. Fattah witnessed al-Otaibi personally behead two Iraqi soldiers as well as being the one who struck a match igniting a gasoline trail into a cage containing a captured fighter pilot that shocked the western world.

Sitting to both sides of al-Otaibi, were two older males who Fattah had seen around the camp, but he did not know their standings in ISSI initially. No one else was in the tent. The instructor bent his head slightly towards al-Otaibi and the other individuals before turning and leaving the tent.

"Sit my brother," said al-Otaibi, motioning to the end of the carpet opposite his position. "Are you hungry?" he asked, as he handed a large bowl containing dates and what appeared to be pieces of goat cheese to Fattah.

"Thank you," said Fattah and he grabbed the bowl and started to remove a few items to eat.

"Your instructors are very impressed with your training Abdel. They tell me that you are far superior to the other recruits. Allah be praised."

The other two males in the tent raised their hands and arms heavenly in agreement with al-Otaibi.

"Do you have any idea why I have summoned you to my tent?" he asked.

"No," said Fattah.

"Before I tell you my brother, perhaps you can tell my friends here a little bit about your prior life before you found Islam."

Not sure what this had to do with his training, Fattah paused and asked how far back he needed to go with his life story.

"My brother, we know that you were once a Christian, is this not so?" asked al-Otaibi.

"Yes, I was raised by my mother and father as a Christian as well as my brothers and sisters. We attended a Christian church in my city. I was unaware of Islam and it was forbidden by my parents to investigate any faith other than Christianity. I married a Christian woman and we have three children. The Americans killed my mother and father in a bombing raid. They were innocent of any wrong doing, but they killed them anyway. It was then that I started to study Islam and found Allah."

With this final sentence, Fattah decided to wait to see what other questions or information al-Otaibi and the other two individuals wanted to inquire.

"Yes, my brother, you too have suffered from atrocities brought upon us by the infidels of the West and with Allah's help, we will continue to strike back at them until we have what we want, a global caliphate secured through a global war," said al-Otaibi, whose words again received a response of outstretched hands for the other two sitting at his side.

"Abdel, I understand that you were born and raised in Ethiopia. Is that not so?" al-Otaibi asked.

"Yes, I was born and raised in Ethiopia's capital city called Addis Ababa. We lived on the outskirts of the city, not in the main part. Is there a mission you wish for me to complete in Addis Abada? I feel that I am ready for whatever Allah commands," he said.

"All in time my brother, but first a few more questions," al-Otaibi responded. He then looked at both men at his side. Without asking a question of them, they both, almost simultaneously, nodded in agreement to some prior arranged discussion.

"I must ask you to return to the time in your life when you are an infidel. I know this may be painful for you, but God has a purpose for your memories. While you were a Christian, did you ever visit Axum?" al-Otaibi asked.

"Axum? Yes, I visited Axum on a few occasions with my family. This was when I was much younger with my mother, father, brothers and sisters, and when I was poisoned by Christianity in my heart." Fattah began perspiring and feared that this line of questioning was now more of an interrogation regarding his true belief in Islam.

"Abu Habib al-Otaibi, please know that my allegiance is with ISSI and Allah. My old life I despise. I am a devoted warrior of Islam. Please do not judge me for the life I have previously lived after being indoctrinated at a young age to a false religion." Fattah felt embarrassed since he believed his response to the three men showed fear in his voice.

Al-Otaibi raised both his hands motioning to Fattah to stop his discourse. "Abdel, we are not here to question your loyalty. The purpose of my questions will soon become apparent, but let us continue."

Feeling a little relaxed, Fattah stared at the three men and waited for the conversation to continue.

The man to the right of al-Otaibi leaned slightly forward and asked Fattah why he and his family went to Axum on several occasions.

Still sensing some fear, Fattah responded, "In the town of Axum, there is a chapel, a building in which the Christian infidels house a supposed religious relic."

The three men looked back and forth at each other and appeared to become very interested in what Fattah was starting4t0o explain. Now he knew what the three ISSI leaders where interested in. They wanted to know about the Ark of the Covenant.

"Tell us what you know about the chapel and this relic my brother," said al-Otaibi.

CHAPTER 6

Frank took a seat upfront in the lecture hall. He estimated that the hall could hold at least 150 students if all seats were occupied. The hall was arranged like a movie theater, with the podium strategically located off to his right, giving every seat an unobstructed view of the huge screen that covered the entire back wall of the stage.

The screen displayed "*Biblical History 1A*," and the professor who would be conducting the lecture, lecture number three, would be a Dr. Nancy Bell. Of course, Frank had inside information about the famous doctor, having been dating her for some time now. He was here today, not to give her some support, since she did not need any, but to get a better understanding of the subject matter that would be a big part of selling the "job" to the rest of his crew, in a few months.

Ten o'clock hit and still no professor. He knew that she preferred to be a little late so that students who either overslept or were just plain lazy, would have enough time to sneak in and get a seat before she started. She abhorred having students come in late when she was at a crucial point in her lectures, and the associated movement and noise creating distractions, causing her to lose some of her students momentarily. Today was no exception, since, even when Dr. Bell walked towards the podium, students rushed to their seats. Most students, Frank observed, were in their early to mid-twenties, although there were a few that looked older and he figured they must be graduate students. Another possibility was that they were there just to scope out Dr. Bell, who was gorgeous in all ways. Frank could not help but feel a sense of ego rising inside, since these students could scope all they want, but the fact was, Nancy was his and his alone.

Wearing a black Gucci pants suit and blue blouse, Nancy was stunning. She started to walk to the podium but quickly looked at Frank with a smile on her face. My favorite student, she thought.

Reaching the podium Nancy said, "Good morning," Some replied in a like manner, but most were too busy looking at their cellphones or readjusting themselves in their seats for what would be a three-hour lecture.

"Remember to please shut off your cellphones, or if you are expecting an "emergency" (which she emphasized but making quote marks with her two hands), put your phone on vibrate. Thank you." Nancy then picked up her presenter and after clicking the devise, pointed to a new slide displayed on the screen.

"Today we will be examining a relic near and dear to my heart. I have spent most of my academic life, when not lecturing (she paused for a laugh), researching this object. Most of you, thirty-six years ago, (1981) were not born yet, and therefore could not have seen the premier of this film, (slide advance) ***Indiana Jones–Raiders of the Lost Ark***."

Nancy could hear, as well as Frank, many of the students say to the people seated next to them, that they saw it, and how it is, an awesome movie.

Nancy continued, "The film was directed by Steve Spielberg from a story by George Lucas, creator of the ***Star Wars*** films and Philip Kaufman (next slide). The film was produced by Lucasfilm Lt.D. and, for those who have never seen it, pitted our hero, Indiana Jones, played by Harrison Ford, (slide advance) against a bunch of ruthless Nazis who, like Indiana, were searching for the Ark of the Covenant. Of course, the bad guys, had different reasons for finding the Ark, since this guy (slide advance), Adolf Hitler, believed that possession of the Ark would make his armies invincible."

Sensing that she had a captive audience, Nancy finished up with the fact that the film was released on June 12, 1981 and became that year's top-grossing film and is still one of the highest grossing films ever made. With that, she paused (next slide).

"Ladies and gentlemen," she looked down at Frank, giving him a sly wink, "this is a drawing, or rendition if you like, of what the Ark of the Covenant is supposed to look like. Its dimensions are approximately 131 x 131 ×79 × 79 cm or 52 × 31 ×31 inches, for you non- metric individuals (laugher in the hall). Various documents state that it is covered with gold inside and out."

A student's hand raised and Nancy acknowledged him. "Professor, what do you think that Ark would be worth today in U.S. dollars?

Nancy responded with, "I really have no idea. How much is gold worth an ounce now-a- days she asked, not expecting a direct answer? Let me just say, that any person who finds the Ark, would have more wealth and prestige than a person could use in a lifetime." Again, she looked at Frank with a smile on her face.

"Let's continue, shall we?" Nancy advanced to the next slide. "According to the Bible and other documents that I have read, most agree that the existence of the Ark goes back to the time of Moses. The Old Testament describes Moses gaining release of the Hebrews from an Egyptian Pharaoh. There is still a lot of academic debate as to the name of this Pharaoh, and that could be the subject of another lecture, later. Suffice to say, that most biblical historians, in their research, shows Moses separating the Red Sea to escape the pharaoh's charioteers after he changed his mind about their release. Moses, with the involvement of God, separates the Red Sea, allowing the Hebrews to escape to the safety of the other side, and then closing over the pursuing Egyptian charioteers.

Moses then climbs Mount Sinai, the mountain of God, and received the Ten Commandments from God, writing them onto two stone tablets." Nancy paused, took a drink of water from under the podium, looked out at the crowd and added, "I want to point out that there are many variations of what I have discussed, and what I am using for this lecture, are those points of reference, that most scholars agree on. But remember, like you not being there for the showing of Indiana Jones and the Lost Ark of the Covenant, I was not born, when these "events" were supposed to have taken place." Most of the students laugh with this comment.

After taking another cup of water, Nancy said, "continuing,"

"Excuse me, professor," a male student stated while raising his hand.

"Yes," Nancy answered.

"I'm sorry, but I am an atheist and feel that most of the stuff found in the Bible, Old or New Testament, is a lot of fiction created by various religious orders."

Nancy and Frank could hear a few boos from the audience. She looked in the direction of the boos, and they stopped. The student continued, "I mean, Samson and his hair, the Burning Bush, separating the Red Sea, turning water in wine, raising dead people, and the best, Jesus raising from the dead. Come on!"

Before Nancy responded, she thought to herself, that there is always an asshole in the class that interrupts her from being on a roll. Today, would be no exception. Some smart ass that feels self-righteous in taking on the professor. Ok prick, bring it on.

"You make a good point." She did not ask for his name in directing her response. Each semester she has over 600 students and found that it was senseless to try to remember their names, since they would move on in their academic career and she would not have contact with them again, so why make the effort.

"I could ask all of you, who believes in God? Or, instead, I could ask who of you believe in ghosts?

Some students, who perhaps were not paying attention, raised their hands, thinking that the professor was asking a question versus something rhetorical.

"The point that I am attempting to make here is that, what this gentleman just said, is viewed by hundreds of thousands of people, if not more. How can a rational person believe in things that defy belief or scientific evaluation? To use some of your examples, (looking at the student), how could a bush burn without being consumed? How could a sea separate itself in two, allowing the Hebrews to cross? How could a person's hair give you strength? And, as you said, the "best," how could a person raise someone from the dead, and later, raise himself from death? As a scientist, all extremely valid points."

Before Nancy made her response, Frank quickly realized that this point of Nancy's lecture, will be extremely helpful, if he is asked similar questions, when he meets with the Banshees. Although he was not sure of their religious beliefs, he was sure that someone in his group will ask questions dealing with fiction and no-fiction issues.

Nancy, after another glass of water, continued, "Similar questions are asked about people believing in other evidence-sparse phenomena such as alternative medicine, sea serpents, aliens, alien abduction, flying saucers, Yeti, Bigfoot and so on.

A common denominator among these examples is a lack of understanding of what constitutes real evidence. If a believer were to be presented with sufficient evidence, one way or the other, the theory goes, and had been educated to understand what counts as "real evidence," then they could be persuaded not to bother with, let alone rely on, whether they should continue to have their beliefs. Psychologists have explanations for the above beliefs involving cognitive errors, frequency illusion, illusory correlation, availability heuristic, bandwagon effect, you know, if a lot of people believe, then who am I to dis-believe, and so on. The scientific method was largely developed to help us counter these universal human tendencies toward making errors in our thinking.

But, when it comes to religious beliefs, well, it becomes a whole new ballgame. Scientific and philosophical arguments rarely work. So, it is not enough to propose to a god-believer or a ghost-believer, "You don't have enough evidence, so, it is not enough to be correct in your belief. Instead, they are convinced that they are right, that they "just know," and there is no clinching evidence that you could offer to change their mind.

Now then, if logic and evidence do not explain the almost worldwide belief in some higher power, God for example, then it must be us; human beings, to "*want*" to believe in it. There must be some internal drive or urge or some innate cognitive tendency toward such belief.

Almost every culture I have ever studied, has included god-like element, even though there is a lack of any substantial evidence. So, we come back to the question, like your fellow student asked, why do people believe in gods? In my opinion, if that is worth anything, it comes down to a psychological need that many of us share, and because of that, we can therefore answer it both psychologically and scientifically.

Psychologist and many scientists feel that our desire to believe in a supreme being, stems from our fear of death. We all know that we will not live forever and that death is inevitable, although we want to avoid it as best we can. This emotion of fear of dying and the motivation to avoid it, is present in all higher organisms. So, many believe, knowing we will all die someday, we are quick to believe in an afterlife where we will be reunited with our friends and family members. Who won't want to be reunited with our lost loved ones?

Therefore, if we believe in an afterlife, is it a stretch to believe in angels, gods? Could we not then, make a case for a parallel universe, alien beings, and don't forget the dark side; devils, mean leprechauns, haunted houses as so forth.

Religious people still seem to fear and mourn death just as much as atheists do." She could see the student who initially raised the question shake his head, indicating no, causing Nancy to add, "Please realize that I am speaking in the general terms. So, since most humans have a fear of death, that could explain some of the reasons for people having a belief in the supernatural. But, I am getting a little off point. I am the first one to admit, that it makes it a lot easier to believe, when there is something tangible to back it up: evidence. And, that said, let's take a short five-minute break, and return to evidence of the existence of the Ark of the Covenant."

Nancy grabbed her bottle of water, took a sip, and then climbed down from the stage to an awaiting Frank, who had stood, and was stretching. "How am I doing babe?" she asked.

Frank replied with a smile on his face, "Sorry professor, I didn't hear a word you said. I was too busy daydreaming about our next lovemaking session."

CHAPTER 7

Boy, how quickly five-minutes flew by before Nancy was again up on stage and behind the podium. The slide she introduced had one centered word, "Relics."

"Ok, now that we have in essence, stated that humans prefer to have evidence to back up their beliefs with a few exceptions, we will continue our investigation of one of the most famous relics, the Ark of the Covenant. But, before doing so, lets' look at some of the relics that we do have in our possession."

Advancing a slide, Nancy said, "This is the Shroud of Turin. It is a cloth measuring 14 ft. x 5 in × 3 ft. 7 inches. It is kept in a Catholic Church, the Cathedral of Saint John the Baptist, in Turin, Italy. It is cloth bearing the image of a man who many believe is Jesus of Nazareth. It is believed that after Jesus's body was taken down from the cross of his crucifixion, it was wrapped in this, his burial shroud. The shroud is kept in in a sealed chamber and is rarely available for public viewing. (Another slide) In 1988, scientists conducted three radiocarbon dating tests on the cloth and they determined that the cloth came from a period of the Middle Ages, and therefore could not be a cloth the once covered Jesus." Nancy again paused for affect, glancing around the lecture hall. From her students faces, she knew they wanted to hear more.

The next slide had one word, again centered. It read "Oops!"

Recently, scientists revisited the Shroud, realizing that the samples taken for radiocarbon dating analysis, was taken from the edges of the cloth that appeared to be different than where the images appeared. So, with permission of the Vatican, (another slide) a more detailed analysis of the fiber was taken as well as swabs taken from the area that appeared to be blood." She again paused, took a swallow of water, looked at her students; they were mesmerized.

"So, what did this new scientific study find? It was real human blood. The cloth taken away from the edges were from a time of Jesus. The weave of the cloth, was that used during the correct time-period. Pollen found on the shroud, is found in that region of the world. They even found pollen in the area that appeared to be that represented by thorns, to be from a weed only found in Jerusalem.

Now, what does that show?" Nancy asked? "Evidence," one student blurted out.

"Yes," Nancy replied. "But evidence of what? What does this show scientifically? It shows that there is blood on the cloth; that the cloth was made during the time of Jesus with the common weave used. That the person was horrifically tortured before being crucified. We can approximate his size. DNA shows that it was of an Arabic decent. When compared to the New Testament of the Bible, the wounds seem to match up. Wounds in the person's hands and feet; a wound to his side." Again, a strategic pause by Nancy, followed by the question, "but, is it Jesus?"

No answers from the students.

(Slide advance) "This is the Sudarium of Oviedo. Many believe that it is the face cloth that was placed on the recently crucified Christ. It is located in the Cathedral of San Salvador, in Oviedo, northern Spain. It measures 33 inches x 21 inches. There is no image on this cloth. It only contains stains that are visible to the naked eye, although more is visible under a microscope. The history of the Sudarium is well documented, and much more straightforward than that of the Shroud. In other words, we can show, through documents, where the Sudarium was and how it ended up in Oviedo, Spain.

We cannot do so with the Shroud. There are some periods where we do not know where the cloth was, or who possessed it.

The stains on the Sudarium, show that when the cloth was placed on the dead man's face, it was folded over, in other words, it was not folded in the middle. Therefore, the fourfold stain has areas of decreasing intensity.

It is evident that the face of this man in which the Sudarium was used to cover his face, died in an upright position. The stains consist of one part blood and six parts fluid. For you non-premed students, this comes from something called pleural oedema. Human liquid collects in the lungs when a person is crucified. And, a crucified person generally dies of asphyxiation, being unable to raise their body to inhale. If the body subsequently suffers jolting movements, blood and water can come out through the nostrils, as you can see here in this slide." (Slide advance).

"Ok, so from a scientific stand-point, what can we determine? From the stains, we can prove that it is blood. But what else?" Nancy received no replies from the students.

"My question could be, is this the cloth that draped the face of Jesus? And, the correct answer would be "no." "To do so scientifically, we would need a definitive copy of Jesus's DNA. Then we could compare this blood to those of the Sudarium, and well we are at it, compare it to the blood on the Shroud of Turin. Then we would have positive evidence that both clothes contained the blood of Jesus Christ."

(Slide advance) Another center word appeared on the screen; *Maybe?*

"A recent scientific study of the Shroud of Turin and the Sudarium, found that the blood on the two pieces of cloth was blood type AB; a very rare blood type. Further analysis showed that in fact, the blood from the Shroud and the Sudarium came from the same person. When pictures were taken of the Sudarium and compared over the face area of the Shroud of Turin – they matched up perfectly." Nancy stopped and could hear buzzing coming from her students. Even Frank looked impressed.

"Again, can we definitively claim, that these two relics are cloths used to cover the face and body of Jesus of Nazareth? "No," she said. "Again, we do not possess a vial of blood or DNA that we can say categorically, that it belongs to Jesus. Bummer huh?" She got a lot of laughter from her students. Probably a little nervous release she thought. "This would be hard evidence, and so far, we do not have it."

"But, let's take it a step further. What if, somehow, we had a sample that positively came from Jesus Christ. I mean, we have no doubt, it really is his blood. We compare that blood with the blood on the Shroud of Turin and the Sudarium and there is a positive match. Gee, sounds like a CSI television episode in the making.

What do we have? We have positive proof that the evidence left behind on those two pieces of cloth, came from the same person. But there are many more questions to be answered. Was he really the Son of God? In other words, the person who made the images on those two relics, was it truly Jesus Christ?

How would we go about proving that one? Obviously we cannot, but for believers, this would simply be "frosting" on the cake, somehow matching the same t images on the Shroud of Turin and the Sudarium directly to Jesus Christ, because they already believed, before this scientific "break- through."

Taking another drink of water, Nancy shuts off the screen and says, "I could spend the better part of this semester discussing and showing you hundreds if not thousands of relics claimed to be the "real thing," again using her fingers on both their hands to imitate quotes signs. But, fortunately for you, with the invention of computers and the World Wide Web, you can spend hours researching this on your own, in-between studying, eating, sleeping, drinking, partying etc." More laughs.

"Alright, let's take our normal fifteen-minute break." Nancy told them the time she wanted them back, knowing that a few stragglers will come in late again.

"Sorry I took so much time to answer questions. I know you really want me to get to the juicy stuff, right?" she asked.

"Don't say juicy around me. Do you want me to blush in front of your students?" Frank replied. After she winked, he said, "you know, some of those older students in here, are not here for your lecture, Doctor.

She placed her arms around Frank, not caring about some of the "woof5,8 woof " comments made by some of the students who did not leave the lecture hall for the break. "I don't care why they are here or what they are thinking, since I only have eyes for you."

This was followed with a quick kiss on the cheek. More "woof, woofs" could be heard. Now Nancy and Frank were blushing. Thoughts entered Nancy's head, if only Frank knew what was coming.

With the fifteen-minute break actually lasting for twenty, Nancy once again, climbed back up to the podium.

CHAPTER 8

I believe I left off, before my tangent, with Moses returning from his visit on Mount Sinai, carrying two stone tablets that supposedly had God's Ten Commandments written by God himself. God gave Moses orders detailing exactly, how the chest was to be constructed including the cheriums on top (slide advance), and that it would be used to carry the Ten Commandments, as well as other items to be placed in it." Nancy moved to the side of the stage near to Frank. She continued.

"The Old Testament goes on to say that Moses, and the Hebrews, carried the newly constructed Ark through their travels in the desert including into battles that they encountered. Further, the Old Testament and other related documents, explain the "powers" associated with the Ark. What sort of powers you ask?" She waited and then continued, "When the Hebrews approached the River Jordan, the river was at flood stage. God had instructed Joshua, who was Moses' assistant and who took over the Hebrew tribe after Moses died, to have the carriers of the Ark to go ahead of the Hebrews, to the shore of the Jordan River. When they reached the Jordan River, God, would show his power to the Hebrews and let them know that he supported Joshua. Joshua told the priests who carried the Ark, to advance to the shores of the Jordan and then to slowly place their feet in the river. Joshua also told the Hebrews to follow the path of the Ark, but not to get close to it, for they would die. The carriers of the Ark reached the shore, and although frightened, began to walk into the river. At that time, God stopped the flow of water on one end, allowing it to build up until the Ark and the Hebrews made it to the other side." Nancy noticed that her students were spell bound.

"Another event, describing the awesome power of the Ark, was the Battle of Jericho. Moses had instructed Joshua to seize the land by conquest, and placed them under the command of Joshua. The first up was the city of Canaan. The Canaanites lived in fear of Israel and their God, which they carried in the Ark. The Israelites marched around the walls once every day for seven days with the priests parading the Ark of the Covenant. On the seventh day, they marched seven times around the walls, and this time the priests blew their ram's horns. The Israelites began shouting as loud as they could, and the walls of the city fell." Nancy paused and took a drink of water.

"The Ark is said to have unstoppable power. Supposedly, any army or nation that possesses it, cannot be destroyed. It represents God's throne on earth. But, it comes with its risks.

An inadvertent touch of it, even by a man who meant no harm, is struck down by an electric shock so deadly that death is instantaneous. A nation deemed not worthy of its possession, will endure its plagues, disease, pestilence, and other maladies, until those deemed worthy are back in possession of it. The Ark had special handling instructions. It rewarded those who gave it respect and it punished violators. The first to pay the price were Aaron's two sons who got burnt to a crisp for making an unsanctioned ritual near the Ark.

If that is not enough for you regarding the supposed power of the Ark, I have a final story about what happened to the Philistines after they captured the Ark and brought it to one of their temples in the city of Ashdod where they already had standing, an idol of one of their gods, Dagon. The next day, the Philistines found their idol lying face down on the ground, so they restored it to its original position. The second day, the idol fell face down on the ground again; only this time its head and hands were broken off. Shortly afterward, the people of Ashdod fell sick with hemorrhoids."

Nancy continued, "When they sent the Ark to the city of Gath, hemorrhoids broke out there."

"Ouch," said Jessie (Slide advance and another drink of water)

"So, let's take a closer look at what the Ark is supposed to look like. Moses had it constructed of acacia wood to those dimensions given to him by God. It was lined inside and out with pure gold. The lid, known as the Mercy Seat, was also made of gold and has three figures carved into it. One is the face of a lion, the other an ox, and finally, the face of a human. When you have time, you can Google what these meant to the Hebrews. There are some stories that during certain events, the wings of the cherubim (slide advance) turn outwards, allowing for sacrifices to take place on the Mercy Seat," (slide advance).

"The Israelis were well aware of the power of the Ark of the Covenant and what would happen if a person (non-priest) came in contact with it, so, when the Israelis camped for the evening, the Ark of the Covenant was placed in the center of their resting area. It was surrounded by "fencing" made of white linen, except for the entrance. This had brightly colored linen indicating the entrance to the Tabernacle.

Here is a drawing of what it might have looked like (slide advance). Here you see the fencing using cloth. In a straight line from the entrance, once inside, is a bronze altar, followed next by a bronze laver. Before you ask, a laver in biblical terms is a basin for washing. This tent-like structure was known as the "Holy of Holies," and that is where the Ark of the Covenant was kept.

CHAPTER 9

Looking at her watch, Nancy realized that she needed to speed up her lecture if she wanted to finish it today, and she did. She hated when she had to start a lecture of the same subject matter a few days or week later, since she had to rehash old material so her students, who had other classes, could remember where she had left off.

"Ok, time flies, when you are having fun." Nancy looked at Frank who smiled at her remark. "I need to speed things up a little so we can wrap up this lecture today.

Unlike the Sudarium cloth, the Dead Sea Scrolls, and to some extent, the Shroud of Turin, we can pinpoint, using biblical texts and other documents, where the Ark of the Covenant was up to its disappearance. And here is where you "wanna-be" Indiana Jones types might really want to pay attention." She stopped until the laugher subsided.

"We can trace the Ark from its construction and possession by Moses, all the way to King Solomon.

We have texts that stated that the Ark of the Covenant was housed in the Holy of Holies in Solomon's Temple on what is known as the Temple's Mount; in essence, a large boulder. This boulder was used as an altar that the Ark was placed on, inside the Tabernacle.

Now, again, here is where it gets "juicy." She saw Frank smile with her comment.

"When the Babylonians invaded King Solomon's kingdom, many texts state that the Ark was either hidden or moved to a safe location. If you believe it was hidden in a cave or hole in the ground, well, the story pretty much ends as to where the Ark is since, whoever buried it, or placed it in a cave, never left directions as to its location; as least, if there were directions, they have never been found.

Another story has it that King Solomon had a son, after a short relationship with the Queen of Sheba (slide advance), This happened well before the Babylonians invaded. Sheba went to Ethiopia and there, gave birth to her son. When he grew up, and upon learning of his heritage, he returned to the kingdom of his father and announced his birthright. Satisfied that he truly was his son, King Solomon gave the Ark to him to be transported to safety in Ethiopia, (slide advance showing Ethiopia in Africa) before the Babylonian invasion.

There are many texts that describe the razing of Solomon's Temple and of riches removed by the Babylonians, but no mention at all about the Ark of the Covenant." Nancy looked around the room. All her students were looking at the slide.

(Slide advance) "This is Axum, Ethiopia. It is a very small town, some might call it a village. So how does this fit in regarding the supposed present location of the Ark? Well, the Ethiopians claim that the Queen of Sheba lived in their country later in life and not in Arabia as most believe. When her son returned from his father, King Solomon, with the Ark, the Ethiopians knew that they needed to house it in a safe location. There is very little information as to where it was kept.

Now, is there anything written that could prove that this happened; remember, positive proof?" As Nancy said this, see looked in the direction of the atheists' student.

"Entering the picture so to speak, are nine Knights Templars. For you history majors, this is the time of the Crusades. These knights show up in the middle ages, and set up camp specifically on the Temple Mount. Their activities were always secret. Why? Well, some biblical historians and archeologists believe that they set up camp and lived there on that spot, so that they could find the lost Ark of the Covenant and bring it to Rome. They set up tent like structures and fencing to prevent outsiders to see what they were doing. Even though they told everyone that they had been sent there by the pope to guard the main road for travelers coming to the holy city, they rarely left the Temple Mount.

Then, they left. No reason was given by the Knights.

They just left. When locals went to the Temple Mount in curiosity of what the Knights were up to, they found many tunnels around the boulder going in every direction.

So, what were they looking for? The Ark, what else.?" Nancy stopped and realizing that she had no water left in her water bottle, she continued.

"Picking up the trail of the Knights Templar, we find records that the original nine pick up more candidates for knighthood and their membership grew. They traveled from Jerusalem almost directly to Ethiopia and to this town (slide advance) Axum.

This church and this chapel is where my lecture will eventually end today. For you see, the Ethiopians claim that this little chapel (slide advance) houses the Ark of the Covenant. And this monk (slide advance) known as the guardian, protects the Ark and is the only one who can be in possession of it." Glancing around, Nancy saw all her students lean a little more forward while focusing on the screen.

"No one can enter the chapel, not even the hierarchy of the Ethiopian Orthodox Church. The guardian is not allowed to leave the grounds of the chapel and I was fortunate when I visited this site (looking at Frank) to get a picture of him since he rarely comes outside. Is the Ark of the Covenant inside, and if so, where inside? Is it the really Ark, or is it a replica? You see, all churches in Ethiopia claim to have the Ark of the Covenant, but through my research, I learned that what they are referring to, is not the actual chest, but replicas of the stone tablets containing the Ten Commandments.

So, ladies and gentlemen, there you have it. A mystery that someday, may be solved, or not. It is a mystery that has been unanswered for almost 3,000 years. But, as some movie or someone once said, "The truth is out there." Nancy waited for the laugher to die down and then said, "Do not forget, your midterm exam will be next Monday. Approximately 50 multiple choice questions and two short essays on chapters one through thirteen, and it will not be graded on the curve. Have a nice weekend." Nancy looked at Frank who motioned as if he was giving her an applause for a job well done.

Nancy gathered up her written notes from the podium and placed them and her presenter in her briefcase. She folded her Mac laptop and placed it in the padded area of the briefcase, finally closing it with her straps inserted into their clasps. She grabbed her empty water bottle and threw it in a garbage can near the exit from the stage. Starting towards the stairs to meet up with Frank, she saw that her "atheist" student, and another female student, were waiting for her descent.

The "atheist" who got there first stated, "Professor, I must tell you that you really got me thinking about a lot of things, not just about where the hell is the

Ark of the Covenant, but religion and a person's belief system. I just wanted you to know that I thoroughly enjoyed your lecture today."

Nancy told him thank you, and that she really liked the discussion they had. Nancy thought, what a kiss-ass. Satisfied with that response, the "atheist" started to leave, allowing the female student to advance.

"Dr. Bell," the student said so softly that Nancy had to motion her forward since she could not hear due to the leaving students.

"Dr. Bell, I'm a Christian, and I just wanted to say, that your lecture today, put my minister's sermons to shame. I am sure you noticed that you had all of us listening to your every word." She waited for Nancy's response.

Nancy responded, "Well thank you, but I still saw some students paying more attention to their cellphones than me."

"Well, sadly, they missed out on a fantastic lecture. I could not believe that the three hours past so quickly. Anyway, thank you for inspiring me to become a biblical scholar like you."

"Well, thank you for such a great compliment. The field of biblical scholars needs more women," Nancy said, and the female student nodded and walked away. Nancy walked up to Frank who immediately took her briefcase from her. She gave him a kiss on the cheek and said, "Longest three hours you ever spent in a lecture hall?"

Frank had a grin on his face, and said, “Almost the best three hours I ever spent.”

“Almost?” Nancy asked quizzically.

Frank answered, “Yes, it cannot compare to some of our three-hour marathon love making sessions we’ve spend together.”

“Three hours, aren’t you exaggerating a little?” Nancy said, followed by a kiss.

“Just a little,” Frank said, winking back at her. He added, “You must be tired, how about if I take my favorite sexy professor out for drinks and dinner?”

“I would love to, but the university has rules strictly forbidding any intimate relationships with our students,” Nancy replied.

Frank continued the banter with “Not a problem. You see, Dr. Bell, I was only auditing your class. I am not enrolled as a student in this fine institution.”

“In that case, I would love to have drinks and dinner with you, and for dessert, I would like to have….. you.” With that, Nancy grabbed Franks’ left free hand and they left the lecture hall.

Nancy had to make a quick stop at the lady’s bathroom. She did not need to relieve herself as much as wanting to glance at her cellphone. Yes, he called, but she would have to call him back later.

Chapter 10

Ethiopian Airlines Flight 1093 arrived at the Addis Ababa Bole International Airport at 1300 hours on Tuesday. Fattah had only been issued his passport, visa and orders two days earlier. His instructions were simple: Travel to Axum and scout out the chapel and area for a future ISSI attack. He is to make no contact with any family or friends and not frequent any previous locations where his identity might be recognized.

While waiting for his flight and making sure he was not being followed, Fattah was able to use his burn phone and called a number from memory.

"This call is for Mr. Stevens. Please have him meet at our normal location at 1600 hours today. This a priority one meet." He waited for confirmation from the anonymous female who had answered the call and then hung up.

After hailing a cab, he gave instructions to take the Dire Dawa highway towards the Awash National Park. Fattah had been there many times both as a child and father. It was 225 kilometers east of Addis Abada and was covered by over 756 square kilometers of acacia woodland and grassland. He told the driver upon entering the park to proceed south along the Awash River knowing that there was a large waterfall and park benches near the end of the park.

He paid the driver after getting a card from him in case he needed to be picked up later. The driver offered to stay, but Fattah declined his offer. He did not know how long this meeting would take and did not want a cab standing by that might cause attention to the meet.

He found a wooden bench close to the waterfall and using a newspaper he took from the backseat of the cab, acted as if he was engrossed in an article. Instead he periodically glanced to the surrounding area looking for any approaching individuals and trying to see it by chance, he had picked up a tail. He continued this practice until at almost precisely 1600 hours, he saw the person he had requested walking towards the bench but not in a direct manner. He stopped near a gift shop about 50 feet from Fattah's position and lit a cigarette. Fattah knew that he was using the window panes to mirror his surroundings, in hopes of spotting tails before approaching the park bench. Sensing that it was safe to proceed, the man approached the bench.

"Is this part of the bench being occupied?" he asked Fattah.

"No, it is not," came the reply at which point Fattah slide a little farther to the end of the bench creating a little longer distance between him and his handler.

Taking another cigarette from a pack he had removed from his pocket and lighting it, the handler said, "Nice seeing you, but we are very surprised to not only hear from you but now find you in Ethiopia. This must be urgent?"

Fattah opened the newspaper again and when he turned his head to the side of the paper nearest his handler. "Yes, this is urgent and is as much of a surprise for me as it is for the agency. I was summoned to a conference with al-Otaibi five days ago," he said. Before he could continue, he was interrupted by a question.

"Al-Otaibi was at the training camp himself?" "Yes, he was there with Gulmurod Khalimov and Abu Yusaf. They were still there when I was driven to the airport this morning," said Fattah.

"Jesus Christ! To our knowledge these three top level assholes have never been together. They must be planning something big." The handler paused after realizing that he was perhaps speaking to loudly although there was no one else around and the sound from the waterfall would probably mute out most of his conversation to anyone further away than Fattah. "Yes, it was hard for me to contain my shock when I entered the tent and saw the three of them together. Part of me worried that someone at Langley would order a drone attack while

I was with them." Fattah stared at his handler after making this comment but saw no reaction.

"So, why are you here? I assume it has something to do with the meeting you had with them," the handler asked while glancing around the park.

"What do you know about the Ark of the Covenant?" Fattah asked.

"You mean like the Indiana Jones Raiders of the Lost Ark?" the handler replied.

"Yes, the Ark that was constructed by Moses and contains among other things, the actual stones engraved with the Ten Commandments: that Ark." Fattah stated while watching a young mother advance pushing a stroller.

After the mother and stroller passed, the handler said his only knowledge of the Ark was what he learned from the movie. He did not think it was real, just something made up by Hollywood.

Fattah continued the conversation. "No, to Christians the Ark actually existed and was constructed by Moses by orders from God. It is supposed to be covered in gold and has immense power, but, it's location after the time of King Solomon, has been lost. There has been speculation over thousands of years as to what happened to it and where it might be."

"Ok, so why is this relic of importance to ISSIs?" the handler asked, interrupting Fattah.

"After he questioned me about my knowledge of the Ark, al-Otaibi wanted to know about a chapel located in Ethiopia that claims to possess the actual Ark."

"You mean, the Ark of the Covenant, the actual Ark, still exists?" the handler asked.

"According to the Church of Our Lady Mary of Axum, yes, it does exist and has been in their possession guarded by the Church. The catch is that no one other than a monk, known as the guardian, has actually seen it. It is locked up in a small chapel. Look, I could go on and on about the supposed possession of the Ark by the Ethiopians, but I contacted you to inform the agency of what ISSI is planning."

"I am still a little confused. Why is ISSI interested in the location of this Ark thing? They hate Christians and Jews. How is the Ark going to further their desire for a world caliphate? "

Fattah explained. "According to al-Otaibi, since I asked a similar question, the Ark of the Covenant is a holy relic to both the Jews and Christians. To ISSI it is a win-win situation. If they hit the chapel and the Ark is not there, they blow up the chapel, kill the guardian and anyone else who gets in the way, and shock the world with another act of terrorism.

But, if the Ark is there, they can ransom it for who knows how much money, forcing indirectly, the Jews and Christians to finance further terrorist acts." Fattah paused so that his handle could process what he had just said. In other words, according to al-Otaibi, Christians and Jews use the Old Testament in their worshipping. Even though Christianity is related to the birth of Jesus and he is not a part of the Old Testament, there still is a support of the Jesus connection to God and the resurrection and on and on. In the Catholic faith for example, references are made between both the Old and New Testament. They are linked. If ISSI does find and take the Ark and either keeps it for ransom or decide to destroy it like they have been doing with religious and historical statues, they can deny Christians and Jews a link that supports their beliefs.

CHAPTER 11

Upon the conclusion of the meet, the handler gave Fattah a burner phone and told him to return to his hotel until further instructions.

Fattah had already arranged for a single night stay at the Ambassador Hotel in Addis Ababa. He was instructed by al-Otaibi that upon arrival in Addis Ababa, to stay one night at a hotel and then set out early the next day for Aksum. Once in Aksum, he would blend in with the locals and attend two days of pilgrimage around the chapel and adjacent buildings. While conducting his reconnaissance, he was to take as many pictures as possible without creating suspicion. Upon completing his mission, he would return to Addis Abada and take the earliest flight back. This information was shared with Fattah's CIA handler.

"Ok, go back to your hotel. You will receive instructions on how to proceed in a few hours. You were right in contacting me." After stating this the handler lite another cigarette and walking in the same direction the lady with the stroller used earlier. Soon he was out of sight.

Fattah picked up the folded newspaper containing the phone and walked in the opposite direction. When he was a few yards away from the park bench, he used the phone to call the same cab driver from earlier. He arrived back at his hotel and went directly to his room. He took a long shower and decided to order room service instead of venturing outside again. He thought about a chancing a call to his family but decided against it. It would be stupid to do something so dumb and not only risk his safety but that of his family. Instead he decided to turn on the news and relax on the bed. He did not have to wait long for the phone call.

Without identifying himself, Fattah recognized his handler's voice which said, "Proceed with your previously given plan. Once you return from your destination and prior to departing, contact me for an update. Good luck." With that, the handler hung up before Fattah could have said anything if he needed too, but he had nothing to add.

At 0700 hours the next morning, he left for the chapel. With no flights to the region, he was relegated to taking a bus like most pilgrims for an 18-hour drive to the chapel location depending on if the bus made it without breaking down, which was a normal occurrence that he recalled from his earlier trips to the region.

Upon arrival, he found a cheap motel room, registered, and immediately began blending in with the hundreds of pilgrims who seemed to arrive constantly. He began taking pictures and was flooded with many memories of traveling to the holy site both as a youth and adult. He had only caught a brief glimpse of the new guardian of the Ark and realized that this person was not the one he had seen as a child. That person seems very old and had an extremely hard time walking to the gate to retrieve groceries and gifts left by pilgrims.

Fattah limited his interactions with other pilgrims to the exchange of pleasantries hoping that he would avoid the possibility of running into someone he knew. He took pictures around the entire area of the chapel, including the back of the building realizing that it would be an extremely soft target for even a small detachment of jihadists. The thought of the guardian possibly being slaughtered in the most heinous way during the mission revolted him and he hoped that somehow a counter action plan by the CIA or military would preclude it from happening.

The next day, satisfied that he obtained enough intel for al-Otaibi, he returned to Addis Abada and stayed at the same hotel he occupied a few days earlier. The next morning before flying back to Syria for his debriefing, he made a clandestine call to his handler as instructed. He relayed his update at which point his handler told him that the agency felt that the odds were good, that al-Otaibi would select him to lead the assault on the chapel in the future raid. Assuming that would happen, Fattah, upon his return to Addis Abada, should break away from his team and contact his handler again for further instructions.

CHAPTER 12

Frank was already sitting in a booth in the bar nursing a vodka martini with two olives. There had been three, but he already ate one. He purposely chose the early afternoon for the meet, to avoid the large crowds that would fill up the place after they had finished their workday schedule. He was glad that the music playing was low so that he could not make out the lyrics to the rap crap that was playing. Being in his early sixties, he preferred classic rock-n-roll and even some music from the 70s – 80s, but nothing from hip-hop or rap.

The first to arrive was James Fielding, a forty-something blond with a tattoo of a snake on his left forearm wrapped around a dagger. Looking like a middle-aged surfer, he stopped at the door entrance to allow for his eyes to adjust to the darkness. Once he adapted to the dimness, he scanned the area and quickly recognized Frank in the booth. He nodded recognition of Frank as he approached. As mutual gestures were exchanged, the door again opened and a large muscular, slightly overweight baldheaded male walked it.

It was Jessie Hawkins who could easily pass for an NFL lineman. He did not scan the area like James, but instead made a beeline to the bar and placed an order. While waiting, he slowly turned from the bar and saw Frank and James in the corner booth. He nodded, turned back to the bar, grabbed his beer, made payment, and walked to the other two. He shook Frank's hand, but exchanged a modified handshake with James requiring them to shake, bump, and tap the top and bottom of their hands.

Frank did not seem amused but did ask in jest if this was some secret gang handshakes? Both James and Jessie laughed and said that Frank needed to get out more. Being only a few years younger than Frank, Frank replied, "Yeah and you wish you were in your forties, don't you?" Even though Jessie was huge compared to Frank and James, he could squeeze in on the same side with James, across from Frank.

James was the newest member of Frank's team. He did not have military experience and was not highly trained as the other Banshees. Frank met him at a sports equipment show in San Francisco, being introduced by Ed who had met him at a local gym. Looking like one of the original Beach Boys, Frank started up a conversation as the two of them were examining killing knives.

James was recruited into the Banshees after Frank learned that his job was in custom control at the local ship yard. One of the hardest things for returning veterans was how to get contraband pass customs. Bringing James into the group eliminated that problem. Frank, using his contacts in Afghanistan, would arrange for a shipment of "goods" to arrive at the custom yard. He would arrange for the contraband to be at the very end of the trailer so that, when the doors were open, the goods would be the first off loaded.

Frank would relay the information regarding the shipment to James who would covertly open the trailer, remove the property and transfer it to a waiting van. Frank would take possession and divvy up the profits. Shipments continue to arrive long after the war had ended with Frank arranging with his contacts in Afghanistan to ship the massive amount of lout his team of Banshees had stolen during the war. When he found a buyer in the states who were interested in purchasing weapons, drugs, or other valuables, an "order" was place to his contacts and the shipment process began.

This conversation expanded into the type of music each liked, with Frank being surprised that James preferred classic rock-in-roll. They had a hotdog and Coke together will looking at speed boats and small yachts. Frank learned that James had attended professional yachtsmen training at a school in Florida but ran out of money before graduating.

"So, what's going on Sergeant?", Jessie asked, but before Frank acknowledged the question, the entrance door opened again, and another male entered the bar.

It was Ruben Morales. About Frank's age, he was still in good shape and always alert to his surroundings. His dark Mexican hair was pulled back into a ponytail and he wore a vintage red and gold Pendleton shirt. He removed his Wiley X Romer 3 sunglasses and placed them in his left front shirt pocket.

"Gee Sarge, what are you doing, bringing the whole squad together again? Must be a big job huh?" asked Jessie.

"Hey guys, what's hanging?" asked Ruben as handshakes were exchanged.

"Have a sit and as soon as the rest of the team gets here, I will let you know what is going on," Frank said. Next to arrive was Ed Martinez and Joe Rivera. "You guys been here long?" asked Ed. These were the last of the Banshee team.

Ed was in his late fifties and showing rapid hair loss, but sported a thick goatee sprinkled with patches of gray. Part of his left ear at the top was missing. He tried to cover it by letting his hair grow long and combing it over this ear.

Joe was the shortest of the five now sitting in the corner booth, but he made up for this by displaying a body chiseled from marble. His biceps would make some body builders jealous. He had a large dropping mustache and piercing green eyes. He also displayed two small rings in his right earlobe and a what appeared to be a diamond stud in his left. A ponytail was lying down his neck and looked pretty long. He too, was in his fifties.

Before anyone spoke again, the barmaid must have realized that the group at the corner booth might leave a hefty tip, so she moseyed over and made sure she moved her hips in a seductive way. She had already unbuttoned a third of her blouse to give the guys something to look at.

"Hi guys, what can I get for you?" she asked.

Everyone placed their orders, including Jessie, who gulped down his beer and handed the empty glass to the waitress. After getting their orders, she retreated to the bar. At that time, making sure no one was watching, Frank reached under the table and retrieved a briefcase that he brought in when he arrived. Cautiously he opened the briefcase and took out five envelopes. He handed each of the five, an envelope and when completed, stated, "we each made $50 large on our last heist."

"Yeah, that's what I'm talking about," said Jessie.

Frank looked at him and Jessie knew that Frank did not want attention to fall on their little group. He told everyone to put their envelopes away and that the first round of drinks was on him. They all did as was instructed.

"Has anyone kept track of how many jobs we have pulled, since the war I mean," asked Ed. "Sorry James, but you came late to the party, so that is why I am using our Special Forces time as my date."

James did not wait for either Frank, or anyone else to answer, but instead said, "For me, this last job was number six, and I hope there are more to come."

Joe was the next to speak. "Shit, I don't know Ed, maybe twenty-five – thirty. Do you know Frank? I mean, does anyone keep a record:" No one answered because of what happened next.

For a fourth time, the entrance door opened. Even the barmaid had her mouth open as she looked at the female entering the room. Initially her body was outlined by the outside light, and with that illumination, it was striking. And, when the door shut and everyone's eyes could refocus on the female, it only got better. She was carrying a briefcase, but only Frank noticed.

Nancy, 5 feet, 7 inches tall, raven black shoulder length hair, wearing a dark blue form fitting business suit, stood near the closed door. The more focusing everyone did on her, the more they realized that she had a super-model figure.

Like Jessie, once she located the bar, she avoided eye contact with anyone else, and walked directly there. The bartender stammered for words and only after he cleared his throat, did he get the question out, "What would you like?"

"Screwdriver", she replied.

She grabbed her drink and told the bartender to put it on the tab with the group at the corner booth, motioning in the direction with a nod of her head.

She then turned, and walked directly over the large group. The bartender continued to watch her walk to the booth. What a fox he thought.

Only Frank gave a "hello." Only Ed stood at her approach.

She smiled at Frank in a more than pleasant courtesy way, then she glanced at the other males seated across from each other. Ed, realizing he was the only one standing, sat down.

The barmaid quickly grabbed a cushioned seat and brought it over to the end of the table, saying to Nancy, "Here you go honey."

Nancy smiled and slid into the seat, placing her screwdriver on the table and briefcase at her feet. Still, apart from Frank's "hello," no one spoke. Instead, the other males in the booth continued to ogle at Nancy. The only one who seemed to not pay much attention was James.

The barmaid, now realizing that her tip was shrinking due to the stunning competition that just added to the number of people at the corner booth, still took drink orders, causing the stunned males around the table to finally speak. Nancy declined and stirred her screwdriver.

Once completed, the barmaid left, knowing that none of the males were watching her retreat. She could wriggle her ass as much as she could, and no one would notice.

CHAPTER 13

"Nancy, since these guys already know each other, I will introduce them to you," Frank said. He was interrupted from saying anything further by Ed, who said, "Hi I'm Ed", sporting a huge smile, showing his bleached white teeth, and offering his hand.

"Hello Ed," Nancy replied smiling, returning the handshake.

"As I was saying", Frank continued, "This is Joe, James, and Ruben, and this big guy is Jessie." No one wanted to lose out on shaking her hand.

"Hello everyone, as Frank has already said, I'm Nancy."

Most of the gang made "hi Nancy" responses, but, not to be out done, Ed chimed in with "it's really nice to meet you."

Frank looked at all the males and said, "are we done with the flirting?" Sheepishly, with their eyes focused on either the table or their drinks, they all shook their head yes.

"Ok, I asked each of you here to not only give you your cut from our last job, but to discuss something else. Sorry it took so long, but getting that much money into the states takes a lot more arranging than bringing in weapons if you can believe it. The other reason I wanted to meet with you is to see if you are interested in a new job, a bigger job than anything we have ever done?" Frank motioned them to lean forward towards each other, while surveying the surrounding booths to make sure no one could overhear his conversation. Before he could start his next sentence, the barmaid arrived saying, "Ok gents, here you go." Drinks were placed on the table and a few men offered a "thank you,", upon which she took the cue that the group wanted privacy, and left.

Frank said, "Nancy, has a Ph.D. in both Biblical history and Archeology, plus a ton of other degrees, too many to name. She most recently, was a professor at the Hebrew University in Jerusalem."

"Wow, intelligent and well as beautiful," said Ed. "Nancy did not blush but did offer a thank you directed to him.

Frank did not say anything, but his glance directed towards Ed, brought on the same results as a verbal mocking.

"Nancy," Frank said, nodding as an invitation to take over.

Nancy reaching with her right hand, pulled up her briefcase and placed it on the table. Frank noticed how his team tried to get a look down Nancy's blouse and it appeared, that they were not disappointed at what they saw, even with it being momentary. Nancy pulled out a single piece of 8 ½"x 11" paper having a colored picture in the center.

Everyone leaned forward, but it was obvious to everyone, including James, the youngest of the group except Nancy, that the picture was that of the Ark of the Covenant.

"Hey, Indiana Jones, Raiders of the Lost Ark, I saw that movie," James said.

Nancy just smiled, knowing that this comment was probably going to be made by someone sooner or later.

"Yes, James, isn't it? I'm terrible with names." Not waiting for his reply, Nancy went on. Most non-religious people, or those that are not Jewish or Christian, became aware of the Lost Ark of the Covenant, due to the Indiana Jones movie, and the movie portrayed a pretty accurate rendition of what many believe the Ark of the Covenant looked like." Before she could continue James asked a question.

"You said what the Ark looked like. I thought it was make believe?"

"I have to say that I also didn't think there was any truth in the Ark, since, like a lot of stuff in the old Testament, it is hard to believe. I mean, parting of the Red Sea and all" said Jessie.

"Guys, let Nancy continue," Frank requested. They all obeyed as if it was a command given in the field.

"Ok, let me just say this, I have spent most of my academic life researching for historical accuracies of Biblical events and locations, listed in both the Old and New Testament. I am also fascinated in religious relics and their present locations. Some of the writings in the Bible I admit, you must take on faith alone. For example, how do you authenticate the burning bush incident unless, God decides to show it to you personally. The same can be said about the parting of the Red Sea or even the resurrection of Jesus.

"Sorry, Nancy, for interrupting, but what's the difference between the Old and New Testament. I wasn't a damn altar boy, so you need to fill me in," said Ed as he quickly glanced at Frank to see if he would receive a reprimand for interrupting Nancy. Frank did not show any anger, so Ed felt at ease.

"The Bible is broken into two sections. The oldest is called the Old Testament and covers events before the appearance of Jesus Christ. To keep this brief, the Jewish faith is based on the Old Testament, while the New Testament celebrates the birth of Jesus of Nazareth and includes his ministry, death on the cross, resurrection and so on." Nancy looked at Frank to see if she had said enough for Ed. The look that she received from Frank, told her that she could move on.

"Oh, so that is why the Jews do not celebrate Christmas and Christians do. I get it now, "said Ed.

"Ok, as I was saying, Nancy continued, "the discovery of the Dead Sea Scrolls, a collection of some 981 different manuscripts discovered between 1946/47, 1956 and 2017 in 12 caves, are of great historical, religious, and linguistic significance because they include the second-oldest known surviving manuscripts of works later included in the Hebrew Bible canon. They are tangible. You can touch them." "Sorry, shall I go on?" she asked Frank.

Frank glanced at this watch and looked around the table. Some continued to hang on each word Nancy spoke, even though she was not speaking, instead waiting for Frank's response. Others looked at Frank expressing that yes, please allow Nancy to continue.

Frank looked at Nancy and said, "go on." Nancy nodded.

"The Shroud of Turin is another example, where the study of an actual object could result in verification of the Crucifixion, death and resurrection of Jesus Christ. Another would be the Sudarium of Oviedo, the supposed cloth that both tradition and scientific studies claim, was used to cover and clean the face of Jesus after the crucifixion.

Some of those relics I just mentioned can be traced over centuries in which we can show ownership or, in the case of the Shroud of Turin, we can use carbon-14 dating and pollen examination, to determine if the relics came from the correct time period or region and so on.

With this (pointing to the picture of the Ark of the Covenant), we cannot do so," she stopped.

"What do you mean?" asked Ruben.

Nancy responded, "The Ark has been documented to be in someone's possession until it was lost after being stored in King Solomon's temple. Gee, I wish I had my laptop and could show you photos."

"You can do that later," Frank said. Understanding that Frank wanted her to move on, Nancy did so. "The Ark of the Covenant, according to several historical documents, disappeared. There are beliefs that it was destroyed, hidden in a cave, buried in the desert. Some countries claim that they have it, though they offer no proof. It is truly one of the greatest mysteries of all time. Where is the Ark of the Covenant?" With that, Nancy stopped talking, stirred what remained of her screwdriver, and put the picture back in her briefcase.

"So, Frank, why did you bring all of us together again?" asked Joe.

Frank did not respond at first, but looked at Nancy for a long time, then at each of his team individually. He then said, "Nancy and I believe that we know the whereabouts of the actual Ark of the Covenant, and if you are interested, how we can steal it."

With everyone wanting in on the mission, Frank told them to meet in two weeks for a more in-depth review of what he and Nancy had planned. Frank, ever too cautious, invited the group to meet at his secluded cabin, high in the mountains overlooking Coeur d' Alene Lake, in northern Idaho.

In the corner booth of the bar, silence fell amongst the people who glanced at each other but said nothing.

CHAPTER 14

"Good morning, Tom. What did you learn from your snitch about the Banshees and their meeting yesterday? asked newly assigned Special Agent in Charge Steven Sadecki of the New York office of the Federal Bureau of Investigation. Special Agent Tom McCormick, sat down across from SAC Sadecki and placed his coffee cup on the table between them. "Well, as we suspected, the meet was originally set up to give all of the Banshees their share of the money that we now know was smuggled in from Afghanistan. "Afghanistan?" said Sadecki.

"I think, sir, that I need to fill you in about the events that have taken place before your arrival."

"Yes, I think you should. Just from the bits and pieces I have picked up, it sounds like this group is involved in a lot of shit," said Sadecki who rose from his seat and filled his coffee cup.

Entering the room was Special Agents Jeannie Loomis, Ismael Flores and James Birk. They exchanged greetings with Tom and their new SAC.

"Hey, I am glad that you three are here since I was going to give Steve a rundown of this entire investigation from the start to what we learned yesterday afternoon," said Tom.

"Well, it is a long investigation involving a lot of agencies, so I guess we should start at the beginning," said Jeannie as she looked at the rest of her fellow agents. Jeannie Loomis, next to SAC Sadecki, was the senior of the team. She had been an agent with the FBI for over fifteen years and had been in line for consideration of a posting as SAC in Atlanta until the investigation she was spearheading went south and she stepped on the toes of a powerful congressman who made sure her career would be scrutinized for the rest of her career.

Average build, with blonde hair tied back in a bun, Jeannie's face showed strain from the many years she had been in the bureau. She had tried numerous times to give up smoking, but to no avail. Married and divorced two times, she had given up any ideas of a happy marriage and children. Now in her late 40's, her life was the bureau and the occasional romp in the hay with whoever she found fascinating in a bar. She realized it was risky behavior, but if any of her hook-ups decided to get rough, her 9-millimeter Glock pointed at their naked groin, would be the great equalizer.

Ismael Flores was the quiet member of the team. He estimated that he had five more good years to give to the agency, before pulling the pin and retiring on some sandy beach in Mexico where he still had several relatives. He almost was forced to retire eight years ago after taking a round in the stomach during a bank robbery. He felt that it was through the grace of God, that he survived the shooting and healed from the trauma without any physical restrictions. He still suffered from the occasional nightmare of the incident, but he convinced the bureau's shrink that he was psychologically fit for duty. His wife of almost forty years had noticed an increase in his alcohol consumption since the shooting, but he never drinks when there is a chance he could be called in on a case. Special agent McCormick had been with the FBI for eighteen years having recently transferred from their San Francisco office. Prematurely bald, he gave up several years ago, combing over what few strands of hair remaining, to taking a trimmer and removing all traces. Now he used a razor twice a week and likes what he calls, "the Rock" look after his favorite actor, Dwayne Johnson. Once divorced and now happily married, he and his wife have a 4-year-old boy and newborn daughter.

Everyone filled or refilled their coffee cups except Tom who elected herbal tea. Sitting around the table, Jeannie began with background information, slowing putting together all the characters, connections, interplay, and conclusions they had amassed up to this moment in their investigation.

CHAPTER 15

Opening a thick file, agent Loomis first pulled out a photo of a military unit showing eight individuals in battle dress uniforms.

Four of the individuals were circled. She turned the photo towards SAC Sadecki and identified Frank Silva, and the rest of the Banshees minus those that died in the war.

"This is their leader, Frank Silva, taken during the Gulf War when they were stationed in Afghanistan. The other soldiers (pointing to them) were killed in action. Their lieutenant was killed but not by a terrorist. He was killed by Frank to shut him up about a theft that they were pulling off. By the way, this team is referred to even by their commanding officers, as the Banshees."

"Banshees?" what is that asked Sadecki.

Special agent McCormick jumped into the presentation and said that the name Banshee, comes from Irish mythology where a female spirit heralds the death of a family member before or after that person dies. The Banshee could take on many forms, sometimes ugly and sometimes beautiful and it sings or shrills to announce a pending death or death that has just occurred. The wailing of the banshee was the first warning to a household about a death, even if the person had died far away and news of their death had not yet come.

She could also predict death. If someone is about to enter a situation where it was unlikely they will come out of alive, she would warn that person by screaming or wailing. Hence why a banshee is also known as a wailing woman."

"But these soldiers are males," said the SAC.

"Yes, then when the SEALS, who dislike this Black Ops unit gave them this nickname, the Banshees actually liked the fact that they too, bring death when they approach: and so, the name stuck." After stating this, McCormick new that he had probably overstepped his bounds, and allowed Loomis to take over again.

"This individual is Edward Martinez, as she pointed to his position in the photo. He is our narc. We were running a sting outside of the Bronx when this clown enters with some flat screens he wanted to sell. One thing led to another and he asks if we would be interested in some weapons from the Middle East. We learn from him that he was a veteran of the Gulf War and was part of an elite Black Ops team called the Banshees. We inflated his ego and he continued to give us more information.

"We contacted ATF and they were very interested in what we might gain from this individual so we decided, with the concurrence of the prior SAC, to form a joint task force which also included military intelligence and Interpol.

While in the war, his team, led by Silva, became disillusioned with the military higher-ups and decided that if they were risking getting their asses shot off, why not see if any profit could be made. They started ripping off terrorists and later drug lords and weapon dealers. They were extremely lucky since even on those occasions when the military began an investigation into their activities, nothing criminal could be found.

The only thing that was learned was that their questionable actions always seemed to occur when their lieutenant was absent. He was called in and questioned by his commander and military police components, but they determined that he did not know what was going on. They enlisted him into watching for any unusual activity by his team, and if anything smelled, he was to inform them so that they could take appropriate action. Conveniently, he was killed in action. Martinez said that Silva shot him in the back with a weapon he had taken from a dead terrorist. When questioned, no one knew how the lieutenant was shot. After the firefight, they found him face down with a hole in his back."

"Did you forward this information to the military authorities? asked the SAC.

Loomis responded, "Yes we did, sir, but they told us that it was best if things remain as reported."

"Jesus Christ," said the SAC. "You mean an officer is killed by his own men and the military does not want to have him arrested, tried and convicted?"

"We were told that in all wars, there are some officers killed by their own men, citing incidents in Vietnam to back up their premise. In this case they said, that even if they wanted to conduct an investigation, what would they get? The men involved would obviously cover for each other. There was no evidence left to be examined. The autopsy would just confirm that the victim was shot with a combatant's weapon. What would be gained? They also said that for the first time in a long time, they have a new president that supports them and that the morale of Armed Forces personnel is at an all-time high. Their military budget has vastly increased. The VA hospitals are being overhauled. The last thing the Pentagon would want to do is bring any type of allegations forward during these times. End of story."

"Jesus," said the SAC.

Loomis continued. "We made arrangements with Martinez to deliver the weapons under a bridge where we could easily manage the comings and goings of anyone who might enter the picture unknown to us. He showed up in a van advertising a painting company. Turned out that it belonged to a friend who had nothing to do with the sale of the weapons. It was a "buy-bust" and we took Martinez into custody without any problems.

During interrogation, things started to get interesting. This hardcore Black Ops soldier actually started to beg for a deal since he knew he could not handle a long prison sentence. We started negotiating with him and he opened up.

CHAPTER 16

He told us that the weapons smuggled in came from contacts the Banshee still had in the Middle East. These fully automatic rifles had been seized during one of the Banshee's many off the book raids. They had a cave in the mountains where their loot was stored, but the big problem was how to arrange for its to shipment into the U.S. when the war ended. Money, drugs, artifacts, weapons, they had it all, but property and individuals, including returning soldiers from the war, had to go through customs when they re-entered.

So, Frank set up a network inside Afghanistan with some Afghanis who would, for a fee, protect the loot inside the cave, and arrange for its later shipment into the U.S. The plan was to ship small amounts over time so as not to come under suspicion.

"This photo," said Agent Loomis, pulling it from the file, "is James Fielding. He was not part of the Banshees during the war, but becomes a key person in the criminal enterprise of the group for he was able to fill an important part of bringing in the loot from the Middle East, "said Loomis.

"An importer-exporter, right?" asked the SAC. "Even better," said Loomis. "He works on the docks for U.S. Customs."

"No shit," says the SAC. "So, Frank places an order with his contacts in Afghanistan who arrange for shipment. Frank gets the details of is pending arrival, cargo id etc. and passes it on to this guy (pointing to the picture of Fielding). He goes about his normal duties as a Customs officer until he sees the arrival of the shipping container. Once it arrives he opens the container and removes the contraband. Very slick, very slick indeed," he said.

"That is how it is done," said Loomis. "Doesn't matter what Frank orders, money drugs, guns, it is all processed the same way and until now, they have gotten away with it."

"So, Martinez decides to do a little freelance with James without the knowledge of Frank or the other Banshees, who probably, would kill him if any of them found out. But, unfortunately for him, he went to the wrong fence to arrange the sales of his weapons." Everyone, almost simultaneously, takes a sip of their beverage.

"The information we gleaned from him was so good, we gave him money that would have represented Fielding's cut of the sales of the weapons, so he feels everything went well," and with that, agent Loomis looked at agent Flores.

"Ismael, can you take over with their plan for the heist of the century?" asked Loomis as she looked at Flores.

"Sure," he said. "Sir," looking at the SAC, "this female is Dr. Nancy Harding (handing him a photo). She has more degrees than a thermometer. She has taught at many top universities here and abroad, and recently completed a professorship in Israel. Her expertise is Biblical history, specifically the location of religious relics. She is an item with Frank. The two of them have traveled many times to the Middle East, and Africa always ending in Ethiopia."

"Ethiopia? Don't tell me that this Frank Silva and his Black Ops team have money, drugs and weapons hidden there also," said the SAC.

"No Sir," said Ismael. According to Martinez, Frank and his team, with the assistance of Dr. Nancy Harding are planning on ripping off this chapel." Ismael pulled a picture of a chapel surrounded by a wrought iron fence and passed it to the SAC.

The SAC leaned forward and picked up the photo. Before he could ask what was so inviting to the Banshees to consider breaking into this church, Ismael continued.

"Dr. Harding, according to Martinez, believes the Ark of the Covenant is inside this chapel guarded only by an old monk referred to by the locals as the guardian, whose duty is to protect and guard the relic." With that, Ismael paused for effect.

"The Ark of the Covenant? The actual physical Ark of the Covenant?" asked the SAC. Everyone nodded their head. The SAC spoke again, "You mean the actual chest that is supposed to contain the Ten Commandments brought down from a mountain by Moses? Again, everyone nodded.

"I'm sorry Agent Flores, please continue," said the SAC.

"Yesterday, as you know, we staked out a bar on the west side. We wired up Martinez and sent him in. Here are some photos of these individuals arriving." Flores, with the assistance of Loomis, handed the SAC photos showing the arrival of Frank, Ruben, Joe, Jessie, Ed, James and finally Nancy.

"We were hoping to learn of Frank's next shipment at which time we would sweep down on everyone and make arrests. When Dr. Harding arrived, none of us could figure out her involvement. It did not take long before she dropped a bomb shell.

According to Ed, no one had ever met Dr. Harding except Frank Silva. He introduced her to the group. After her introduction, she took out a photo from her briefcase showing the Ark of the Covenant. Frank told them that they believe they know the exact location of the relic in Ethiopia, in that small little chapel guarded by an old monk. Frank thought that with enough planning and intel, it would be an easy heist worth millions if not more." Ismael stopped and drank some of his coffee. No one spoke for a few minutes.

Finally, the SAC looked at everyone but focused on Agent Loomis. "So, what is our next move"?

Loomis glanced at Agent McCormick who took over the presentation. "Everyone wants in on the heist according to Martinez, but Frank told them that they would meet again at his cabin up in Idaho where they could discuss more privately, everything involved in the plan."

"Where and when in Idaho?" asked the SAC. "Coeur d' Alene Lake, in northern Idaho in two weeks," replied McCormick.

"We already had some agents from our bureau in Idaho check records of the cabin and it is owned by Silva. Unfortunately, the way the cabin is situated, it would be impossible to place surveillance teams close enough to hear and observe. We should be able to spot them arriving in town before they take the drive up to the cabin, so at least we will have that. Otherwise it is up to Martinez and we don't dare put another wire on him this time," said Loomis. "Apparently, Frank is a very cautious individual even with his own team, and they respect him for that.

"Ok, I assume then that it will be a waiting game until the meet takes place, and depending on what you learn from that meeting, you will formulate your next move, correct?" asked the SAC.

"Yes sir, that is the plan," replied Loomis.

"You said you have military intelligence and their military police contingent as well as the AFT and Interpol in the loop. Where do those agencies fit in for now?" the SAC asked.

"Well, sir, at this time, the military said that they would not get involved unless more weapon shipments were going to be smuggled into the U.S. The ATF has also stepped back like the military, but wants an active part once we start wrapping things up, so that they can track any new weapon shipments as well as those that have already been smuggled into the country."

"That is understandable," said the SAC. "As you know, we have no jurisdiction outside the U.S., and I guess that is why Interpol is involved, correct? he asked. "Yes sir, and unless you instruct us to do so, I felt no need to involve the C.I.A."

"Damn right. We don't need spooks involved in this. We are investigating a theft of property, not a spy organization or terrorist group. I also do not feel we need to involve Homeland Security either. Is that understood?" he asked as he looked at everyone. They all shook their heads in agreement.

"What about Interpol? What is their take on their agency's involvement?" the SAC asked.

Loomis responded with, "We will be meeting with some of their senior agents in Washington tomorrow and discus what part each of our agencies will play. They, like us, are waiting to hear more about the plan before proceeding. The fortunate thing is that

Interpol has an office in the Federal Police Building in Ethiopia so they can monitor any activity going on there between now and the meeting up in Frank's cabin." With that said, Loomis waited for her SAC to respond.

"Ok, keep me informed of any new information or breaks in the investigation," The SAC picked up his coffee cup, refilled it, and left the room.

CHAPTER 17

With everyone wanting in on the mission, Frank told them to meet in two weeks for a more in-depth review of what he and Nancy had planned. Frank, ever too cautious, invited the group to meet at his secluded cabin, high in the mountains overlooking Coeur d' Alene Lake, in northern Idaho.

The weather for August was nice. Once a person reached lake level there was no breeze but in the upper elevations where his cabin was located a cool breeze keep the temperature a comfortable 89 degrees. The lake was teeming with skiers, jet skiers, and today, Frank even saw a person trying to parasail. He'd like to try that someday, but being in his 60's, it better be soon, he thought.

The trip earlier down to the lake, allowed Frank to stock the refrigerator with tons of food and beer, knowing how his group loved to eat and drink. Steaks, baked potato, sour cream, corn on the cobb, and a tossed green salad should do the trick he thought for tonight at least. And of course, he could not forget lots of hard liquor for later. The only one who will probably eat like a bird, will be Nancy. It seems, over the time they had been dating, that no matter what she ate, she never put on weight.

He told everyone at the bar to plan for a weekender. A limited amount of information about the Ark's theft was discussed at the bar, thus necessitating this meet. This mission would require more prep time than anything they had ever done before and that included missions the Banshees did in the Gulf War. It would require months, if not a year, of planning to make this work.

The first vehicle to arrive three hours early, was a brand new, shiny red, Jeep Wrangler. He recognized the vehicle instantly and therefore was not surprised by the driver's early arrival. She climbed down from the Wrangler and looked stunning. She worn white shorts and sandals. Her sleeveless red blouse which matched the color of her Wrangler was tied above her stomach, displaying her tight stomach and belly button. He remembered the days when he could display a six-pack. But, those days are gone. He chalked it up to damn gravity.

"Gee, am I the first one here?" she asked? Frank knew she came early on purpose.

After grabbing her purse and small suitcase, she met him halfway up the driveway to the cabin. He took the suitcase from her and before he could turn and start their approach to the cabin, she threw her arms around him and gave him a long passionate kiss. It seemed like a long time since he had Nancy in his arms, but in reality, it was only a few weeks ago, and her kiss brought back such awesome memories. Before he could register all the emotions that were pulsating through his brain, she took off skipping towards the front door.

Frank followed her up the stairs watching her fantastic figure. She really could have been a high-priced model, but the fashion industry seemed to only desire thin-as-rail females who did nothing sexually for him. Yes, it was a cliché, but he knew Nancy's measurement of 35-24-36, were just the right dimensions in his world, and, by the way the other guys, and even the barmaid, acted as if those measurements met their dreams also.

"You really haven't changed anything here, have you?" she asked. She continued to check the place out, not really expecting an answer from Frank, so he didn't offer. She looked playfully at him and took her suitcase and begin walking upstairs to the master bedroom. Halfway up she turne again and blew him a kiss.

Well, I guess she has decided on the sleeping arrangements, Frank thought smiling. Lucky me.

When she walked back down stairs, she found Frank in the gourmet kitchen shaking a BBQ rub on huge steaks. He always liked to cook, especially for her. The bigger the crowd, however, the happier he seemed to be.

"Where's the beer?" she asked as she made her way to the enormous refrigerator. Again, Frank knew that she did not need an answer since she had been to the cabin a few times before. She brought a beer for him also and opening the correct drawer and found the opener. Frank liked imported beer, and some still did not have easy open tops.

Once open, she handed it to him as he dried his wet hands and took the beer. Clinking the beer bottles together, they each took a gulp. Frank, now satisfied that each steak had the right amount of dry rub on them, he put the steaks in the refrigerator and the two headed upstairs. There was still over two and a half hours before the rest of the members should arrive, so why waste time?

Nancy wanted a shower since she had driven three hours to reach the cabin. Frank, lying in bed, turned on the television to catch up on the news. He found it upsetting that the politically correct group, the liberals, had pretty much taken over most of the television channels. He had one channel that he somewhat believed in, with most "mainstream" news media groups spewing left wing dogma. His favorite, FOX, was also starting to slide a little too much to the left for his taste, but until another conservative station was created, he only had FOX news to satisfy his desire to know what was going on in the world.

Most of his knowledge of current events, came from news he got from the Internet. The only newspaper he read religiously was the Wall Street Journal, though that was primarily for stock information because they were not immune from liberal articles.

He heard the shower being turned off and could hear the glass shower door being slid to one side. He imagined that Nancy was now drying herself. He then heard the hair dryer blowing and knew that soon she would emerge hopefully with not a lot on. He was not disappointed when she came out of the bathroom.

Nancy jumped on the bed; her raven hair still somewhat wet and glistening. She wore a silk bathrobe that only went to just below her hips and it was not tied in the front revealing her desirable body. She rolled onto her right side, throwing her left leg over his groin area. That was all it took to get him aroused, and she knew it. Without saying a word, he quickly rolled over on top of her and in the process, removed her robe.

CHAPTER 18

The love making was animalistic. Frank and Nancy seemed to have different types of love-making episodes. Sometimes it was slow, romantic, as if neither he nor she wanted it to end. Other times, it was what they referred to as "down and dirty, animalistic." Sometimes Frank was the aggressor and other times it was Nancy. It sometimes involved a little rough sex, maybe some role-playing, and at least twice, a little bondage.

They never planned in advance the type of sex they would have. Instead, what they had between them was the ability to use body language, breathing, and eye contact, to determine what love making techniques would they participate in. What they both knew however, what that they both wanted to please each other.

Climaxing together, Nancy still sitting on top of Frank, began lightly touching his chest hair and then his St. Michael's necklace. The medal had been given to him by his mother, who had had it blessed by the parish priest, and given to Frank for protection during the war.

Frank, as usual after making love with Nancy, felt totally relaxed and could easily fall asleep, but that was out of the question. She looked down at him, and he looked up at her. Even though their love making session was over, Frank continued to hold Nancy's breasts in his two hands, massaging her nipples. They kissed and finally Nancy placing her head on his chest, while sliding off him, leaving her left leg still over his groin.

"Frank, I know most of the guys that the guys introduced to me were part of your unit in the Gulf War. All of them seemed surprised that you and I knew each other as well as we do."

Frank did not answer since she really did not ask him a question. She went on. "I could read their body language at the bar when they first saw me, that they had no idea you and I have been together. How do you think they will react when they get here and the cat is out of the bag?"

"Most will say congratulations or something similar, but Ed will probably break down and cry" he said as he laughed. She laughed also and pinched Frank on his nipple.

"So, can you tell me something about each of them? I mean, it would be nice to know how you guys met, anything really?"

She waited to see if Frank would respond.

"Well, I guess we have time," as he stroked her back and played with her hair. "Who do you want to know first?" he asked.

"How about Jessie, the big guy?" she answered. "He is huge. How could he ever get into the military? Don't they have weight restriction and physical fitness guidelines and all that stuff?"

"Jessie, Ed, Joe and Ruben were part of my unit in Black Ops during the Gulf War. We all went through Ranger training at different times, and it still amazes me that we clicked from the start when the unit was formed. The squad initially was made up of eight, but three did not make it back alive. Our lieutenant was the first one killed, and I became the squad leader." Frank did not include the fact they he killed their lieutenant.

"Jessie at the time, only weighed about 180 pounds and was in great shape. He did not balloon up to his NFL size until years later, once he got out of the Army. He was wounded by shrapnel in his shoulder and upper right arm, but he still carried the body of our lieutenant back to safety. He got hooked on morphine or morphine-like meds, and that caused his body to swell up. He was even bigger and fatter before, but then one day, he said "bullshit" and went on a weight reduction program, I think using Nutrisystem, and started an exercise regimen. He won a medal for his actions regarding our lieutenant and what he did in that battle, but like most of the team, he does not discuss it often." It did not bother Frank in keeping the truth from Nancy. What would she gain by knowing the actions he and the Banshees took during the war and afterwards. Somethings are better kept private.

Frank stopped and quickly glanced at this watch. This allowed time for another quick kiss from Nancy which he interpreted as a sign to go on.

"Ed may come across as the flirt, and he sure showed that to you at the bar, but don't let that fool you. Out of our team, Ed is probably the most intelligent. He has two master degrees, in what field I can't remember."

"Wow! Two master degrees but he went into the Army?" Nancy asked. She then caught herself and what she had said saying, "I'm sorry, I didn't mean it to sound like going into the military is only for…"

"I know what you mean," Frank said, cutting her apology off. "I was surprised also when I first learned it from him, and I asked him why in the hell, with two advanced degrees, he wanted to go to the desert and get his ass shot at? He told me that when he heard about the atrocities that the Iraqis were doing to the Kuwaitis when they invaded their nation, he felt that he had to respond.

Now I remember, one of his degrees is in Martial Family Therapy. That's right, because he joked about offering "therapy" to any of the Iraqis he met on the battle field."

"Is that where he lost part of his ear?" Nancy asked.

"Yes, in the same firefight when we lost our lieutenant. You can see that he is a little self-conscious about it and thus the long hair and comb over," Frank responded.

"Should I go on?" Frank asked and Nancy, with a low, almost purring voice, said "Yes" as she continued to process the information about Frank's former platoon members.

"Joe can speak four languages. He is one of those rare individuals that has a knack for picking up another language and is very good at even mimicking the appropriate dialect. I know besides English, he can speak Arabic, Spanish, and one other one; Russian. When he was in my platoon, he was the skinniest one of the bunch, maybe weighing 160 pounds. In fact, we use to call him skinny as a nickname, not realizing it at the time, that our nickname for him hurt. When the war ended, I lost touch with him for about three years and when we met again, he looked like he does today. He is like a baby bull, muscle on top of muscle. It just dawned on me, I hope he will eat the food I have. He is pretty particular about what he puts in his body."

"What about James? He is a lot younger than the rest of you, no offense." Nancy asked.

"None taken. Yes, I think James is about your age. The blond hair, if you have not figured it out, is bleached. As I said, he was too young for the Gulf War. I have only known him for maybe the last ten years. We first met at a sports equipment show and eventually became friends. He talked me into joining his gym where I was going to get rid of some of this." Frank grabbed a little bit of fat from his stomach area.

"Just more for me to love," said Nancy as she grab bed the same area of Frank's stomach. Frank could f eel that he was getting aroused again - so could Nancy.

"Hello there, "Nancy said, touching his rising manhood.

"Should I continue?" Frank asked.

"I'm sorry. Yes, please do," Nancy answered as she gave a light bite on Frank's chest.

As we became friends, I learned that James had been pursuing a Captain's License and dreamed of being a private yacht captain, sailing beautiful women and wealthy clients around the Mediterranean." Frank stopped and again looked at his watch.

"Why did he stop? I mean, gee, he would have those beautiful women, wearing the skimpiest bikinis, just to get his attention on those private yachting gigs?" Nancy asked.

"He ran out of money, plain and simple. So, would you be one of those skimpy bikini ladies trying to entice "Captain" James into the sack?" Frank teasingly asked.

"No, he is not my type," Nancy teased back, thinking that if Frank only knew the truth.

"Oh really, what is your type young lady?" Frank inquired.

"I like the mature, intelligent, masculine, sexy type who has some meat on his bones" she responded.

"That's the answer I was looking for," Frank said as he pulled her on top of him.

"Wait a minute, big boy, as she felt his manhood rise. You still have to tell me about Ruben." She could feel that he was still hard and erect, but she knew that if he lost his hardness while talking about Ruben, she could easily help him raise the flag pole again.

"First, finishing up about James, he now works for Customs at the shipyard, inspecting incoming and leaving shipments. The other team members seem to really like him so he was a good fit.

"Ruben was the last assigned to our squad making us a team of eight before the, while you know. Besides being Mexican, he is also part Indian. Two of the guys we lost, used to call him Tonto, and he did not mind. He also earned a medal in the war, but it was for saving the life of a female that the Republican Guard was going to torture and kill in the middle of a shit hole of a town, as an example of cooperating with the Americans." Frank stopped as if trying to remember the details.

"Was she spying for you guys?" asked Nancy. "No, actually she was in the wrong place at the wrong time. Apparently, a day before our squad moved into her town, an American unit treated some of the inhabitants with medical supplies. She was not there at the time, since she had gone to another village to check on her relatives. When she returned, she found the Republican Guard outside the door to her house.

On the ground near her door, a guardsman found a box of cotton and an ace bandage obviously from the west. That was all the evidence they needed to find a person guilty.

We did not know anything about this at the time we arrived. Ruben was scout and entered the area first. The three Republican Guardsmen had already stripped off most of her clothing and had her hands tied behind her back.

They had forced her on her knees and one on them was behind her with a large knife; kind of like a curved machete. By then the rest of the rest of the squad, including me, turned the corner. We saw Ruben quickly remove a knife from his belt, and moving without making a sound, ran up to the three guardsmen and slit their throats." Frank could feel Nancy tense up a little, but then he continued.

It was so surreal. The guardsmen, especially the one with the knife, grabbed their throats and looked quizzically at Ruben, trying to figure out where the hell he came from, as their blood gushed through their hands placed at the site of their wounds.

Ruben, untied the young women and motioned for her to get her clothes.

Joe picked up the medical supplies from the ground that had started the whole event, and speaking Arabic, told another woman to burn it and anything else that was left behind by the other American soldiers. She quickly did as commanded.

We searched the uniforms of the dead soldiers and found some useful information that helped in a future mission, and so the commanding officer felt that Ruben deserved a medal.

When Ruben was awarded the medal, he gave it to a young Kuwaiti boy as a souvenir. This was when the war was nearly over of course." Frank stopped, thinking that he had now answered all of Nancy's questions, but he was wrong.

"None of them is married?" Nancy asked. "Jessie was married for a while, but his wife asked for a divorce when he ballooned in size and got addicted to the meds. They never had kids.

James is too much of a playboy, and I have never known him to have a steady girlfriend for any length of time.

Joe had a beautiful wife and daughter, but three days before Christmas several years ago, a drunk driver t-boned them in an intersection, killing his wife instantly. His daughter was rushed to the hospital but then, something no one wants to do, he had to make the decision to "pull the plug" and terminate his daughters' life."

"Shit," Nancy said.

"Ed does not believe that humans were made to be monogamists. Being attached to only one person, he feels, is unnatural. He will cite examples in the animal kingdom to support his position. He has had a few decent girlfriends, but none stay around very long when they learned that marriage was not going to be a possibility.

Ruben, out of the group, had been married the longest." Frank said.

"Oh, don't tell me his wife was killed also." Nancy said.

"No," Frank said. He got a divorce after coming home unannounced from deployment and found his wife in bed with another woman. He had a hard time handling that, even saying to us, that finding her in bed with another man would have been easier to digest.

Being gone for so long on deployments, and never knowing if your husband is coming home, could cause a lot of women to stray to another man, but to lose her to a woman, made him question his manhood." Frank stopped.

"How long did it take to get over it," Nancy asked.
"A couple of months," Frank answered.

"That's all," Nancy asked.

"Well yes, we helped him get over it," Frank replied.
"How did you guys to that, if I might ask?" with a flirtation look on her face.

"We took him to Las Vegas, to one of those massive hotels. After dinner, we all went to the bar. They were really busy and it looked like it was going to take forever to get after dinner drinks, so we sent Ruben up to the bar with our orders. As he is waiting for the bartender to take his order, a gorgeous lady walks up to him and starts hitting on him. Next thing Ruben knows is that she is asking him if she could buy him a drink? He was flattered and accepted and, when he was about to invite her to our table, she whispers in his ear, suggesting that they go to her room.

He looks at us and give us the thumbs up, indicating that if we want drinks, we need to get them for ourselves, and that he is out of there." Frank stopped and started to chuckle to himself remembering the events that evening, but did not explain to Nancy.

Frank started again, "After that night, Ruben was a new man. Best $500 our platoon ever spent."

"$500! What did you guys do?" Nancy asked. "What?" Frank asked. "We helped our buddy get out of his depressed state."

Nancy, still amazed said, "Yeah, you guys hired a hooker to help your friend out!"

"No," Frank said. "She was a high-priced call girl, and when she got him up to her room, she said all the right things to build up his ego."

"You guys even told her what to say?" Nancy was shocked, but had a big smile on her face when she asked this question. "Pray tell, what did you tell her to say, or do I want to know?" she added.

"You know, the stuff all guys want to hear. You're so big! Oh, my God! Where have you been all my life?!

This is the best sex I have ever had! Your wife was crazy to lose you!" Frank looked at Nancy is such a way that he felt vindicated for his team's actions.

"Does Ruben know this?" asked Nancy.

"No, and you cannot tell him. If you do, we might have to pay another $500 for more therapy." Frank said.

"Oh, give me a break. Come here!" Nancy said as she reached down to help Frank get hard again, which did not take long. "Oh, you are so big! What a stud you are! Oh, my God!" she said.

"Very funny! And no, I am not going to pay you $500."

CHAPTER 19

Frank, looking out the window to the side of the front door, saw two vehicles arrive at the same time. One was a new Ford Raptor 4x4, blue in color, carrying Jessie and Ed. The other was new gray Land Rover, driven by James with Joe riding shotgun and Ruben in the backseat. "The gang is all here." Frank thought.

"Who owns the Wrangler?" Ed asked as he walked around the outside of the vehicle.

"I do," said Nancy coming out of the cabin door behind Frank.

Wearing white short-shorts, barefooted, with a blue tank top and hair pulled back into a ponytail, Nancy looked totally different than the college professor look she had at the bar.

All four guys stopped in their tracks and just gazed at Nancy. Frank felt so proud.

"What time did you get here?" asked Ed. "About three hours ago," she responded.

With that said, Nancy walked to the side of Frank and placed her arm around him. If there was any doubt as to where Nancy fit into Frank's life, everyone now how an answer.

"Come inside and have a cold one. I will start the coals," said Frank and he walked over to the BBQ located on the deck.

"Shit, some guys have all the luck," said Ed as he and the rest of the group started walking up the stairs with their overnight gear. "Shit," he said again. "I thought I had a shot at that."

"Sure, you did little buddy," said Joe responding to Ed while laughing. The others joined in the laughter. When the BBQ was over and everyone had a full belly, even Jessie, Frank asked everyone to join him and Nancy in the Grand-room. There was a large couch that could easily hold the entire group, but instead, Nancy and Frank stood near the front of the group. Nancy had already placed her Mac Air on the coffee table and had it connected to the 84-inch flat screen television. She had already displayed a slide showing the Ark of the Covenant. There would be no audio so no speakers were required.

"Ok, let's get started," Frank said. First, you now know that Nancy and I have become more than friends. We have been dating since the last job we all did together. I met her at one of her author signings at Barnes and Noble. She had an excellent book out with the subject being the whereabouts of relics including that of the Ark of the Covenant.

"Oh, now I get where you came up with this plan," said James. The others looked at James as he spoke with some nodding.

"Together, she and I started to do preliminary research about the Ark. Actually, Nancy had already done the research, I determined if there was a possibility of us being able to steal it."

Everyone laughed or chuckled at Frank's comment although he did not intend it to be a joke.

"Each of you have the skills, experience and talent to pull this off, but before I go any further, Nancy will give us more detailed background information so we are all on the same page." With that he nodded at Nancy.

"Ok guys, I am sorry if some of this is repetitious from the information I gave you at the bar, but if you let me go with the flow, we can get through it faster." No one said anything, with a few repositioning themselves on the couch. Frank remained standing off to the side near the floor to ceiling rock fireplace.

"According to the Bible, the Book of Exodus specifically, and no, I will not be reading Biblical quotes, the Ark of the Covenant was constructed after Moses return from his climb down from Mt. Sinai, carrying two stone tables containing the Ten Commandments written by the hand of God." She clicked on the second slide showing an artist rendition of Moses returning to the Hebrews carrying the two stone tablets.

"The actual dimensions of the Ark for construction was given to Moses from 1G37od. It is 13 x79x79 cm, or, for those that don't like metric system. Jessie raised his hand as if Nancy was asking for a vote, it is 52x31x31 inches. Once it was constructed, it was covered entirely with gold. There are four rings of gold attached to the corners, two on each side, through which poles were to be inserted so bearers could carry the Ark. It also has a golden lid called the kapporest, or mercy seat in Christian translation, which has two golden cherubim whose wings reach out to each other, as you can see here in this slide showing the picture that I showed you before." Nancy stopped and looked at the men in the room. She could tell that she had their attention.

"There are various guesses as to how much the Ark and its contents weigh, but none of it can be determined as factual," Nancy continued.

"What else besides the stone tablets are believed to be inside?" James asked.

"Good question, James, since it might help us come up with an educated guess as to its weight" Nancy answered. "The Old Testament states that besides the two stone tablets, it also contains Aaron's rod and a pot of manna.

"Before you ask the question," at which point Ed lowered his arm, "Aaron was one of the sons of Moses who took over the search for the promised land for the Hebrews after the death of Moses. Some feel that not only Aaron's rod, but the rods of Moses and Joshua are inside the Ark. Regardless, the rods carried by Moses, Joshua, and Aaron, according to Bible accounts, held tremendous power." Nancy looked at Frank to see if she should say more and the look he gave her said not now.

"There are no biblical accounts as to the thickness of the lid, the thickness of the Ark's sides or the bottom. We have no factual information as to the exact design of the lid, but so many ancient pictures show the two cherubim in the position that they are in, causes us to believe that it is so.

Now, if you were my graduate students, I could go on and on, giving you a bunch of knowledge that you would probably never use except on my midterm or final exam, so instead, I want to focus on the travels of the Ark and where Frank and I believe it is today." Nancy clicks on the next slide.

"As I said, after Moses dies, his oldest son, Joshua leads the Hebrew to the Promised Land. More slides. The New Testament refers to the Ark being with them. A later battle with the Philistines, resulted in the Ark coming under their control. More slides. This is all in the Middle East area. The Philistines took the Ark many places in their country." More slides. She was about to tell about the many misfortunes that happened to the Philistines apparently due to their possession of the Ark, but she could see that Frank was monitoring her very closely.

The Philistines eventually gave the Ark back to the Hebrews. The Ark later came under protection of Kind David who placed the Ark in a tabernacle he prepared for it. (Another slide) David was planning on building a temple for the Ark, but the Bible says that God told him to stop. Another ancient war breaks out and King David is forced to flee Jerusalem taking the Ark with him.

King Solomon (another slide) is the next individual that we have in historical documents, showing possession. He built his own Temple, Solomon's Temple, which contained a special inner room, named Kodesh Hadodashim, meaning, Holy of Holies. This is where the Ark was placed.

Now, here is where the mystery begins. In 587 BC, the Babylonians invaded Jerusalem and Solomon's Temple. There is no record as to what happened to the Ark, at least not in the Books of Kings or the Chronicles.

There are a few references, one of them being an ancient Greek notation in the Book of Ezra, that states that the Babylonians took away the Ark of God, but doesn't say where."

Nancy advanced a slide that showed the words, "And they took all the holy vessels of the Lord, both great and small, with the vessels of the Ark of God, and the king's treasures, and carried them away into Babylon."

"Others ancient texts say that the Babylonians carried the Ark back to Babylonia. Others say that it was carried into Babylon and buried. Still others feel that Josiah, the king of Judah, took the Ark, and its' contents and hide it before the Babylonians invaded Solomon's Temple. Others say it is somewhere on the Temple Mount in Jerusalem." More slides followed.

"Still other accounts say that the Ark in hidden in a cave, sealed up by the prophet Jeremiah, who said that the site should remain unknown. We do not know if the mountain Jeremiah was referring to is Mt. Nebo, in what is now known as Jordon. And there is more; it is back on Mt. Sinai, it was seen in heaven mentioned by St. John in Revelations and so on."

"This would be a good time for a break and then we can tell you where we (motioning to Nancy) think it is located and our plans to steal it. So, grab a donut and some coffee and hit the head," Frank said to the group as he walked over to Nancy. "Good job. Do you want some coffee or tea?"

CHAPTER 20

Most of the conversation overheard by Nancy and Frank pertained to the mystery of the Ark. No one intruded on what was obviously a private conversation between the two of them.

"I was right, that you did not want me to discuss all of the death and destruction that is documented to those that were judged unworthy in possessing the Ark?" asked Nancy.

"Yes, I will cover it after we talk about the plan. It is not that I want to deceive them, but with what they have gone through with me in the military and some of our earlier heists, I think they deserved to hear everything first, before we bring in curses and such. Then, they can decide if they want any part of it and the possible consequences, mystical or not."

"Is that what you think it is, mystical? I thought you believed in God? In fact, don't you and I go to the Catholic Church and pray together sometime? You even wear a St. Michael's medal, "Nancy asked.

"I know, and I have a hard time wrestling with the inconsistencies of my beliefs. I mean, I believe in God although I have never seen him. I believe in the saints, angels, the concept of heaven and hell, but for some reason, I can't accept a lot of the stories laid out in the Old Testament as being truthful. Doesn't make sense, does it?" Frank asked.

"I mean, what kind of God allows for the things I have seen in war? And, it is not just war, what about droughts, famine, terrorist's attacks on innocent people. If there truly is a God, why does he allow such things to happen? Again, doesn't make sense, does it. And, by the way, I only wear that medal because my mother gave it to me. I don't believe that some "saint" was protecting me in battle. It was just that my number never came up."

"Yes, what you say does makes sense. A lot of my academic colleagues, also struggle with not only the Old Testament but even the New Testament," Nancy said.

"How about you? Do you buy into the literal words of the Old and New Testament?" Frank asked.

Nancy did not respond quickly, as if trying to choose the right words. Then she said, "I have been asked the same questions by those I work with, you know, about my personal opinion, about God, heaven and hell, Old and New Testament, and especially if the Ark of the Covenant has special powers attributed to it, since they all knew about my intense interest in it. I told them that I'm not a believer in any kind of special power or spirits like Hollywood shows in *"Raiders of the Lost Ark,"* but I am completely opened minded about whether the Ark really existed and of course, the Ethiopian's claim to possessing it in the Chapel of the Tablet in Aksum." She paused and then continued, "there are a lot of people, not just Ethiopians, who believe that the Ark is inside the Chapel. Who am I to say they are right or wrong until I have some positive proof one way or the other? I apply no religious beliefs to the authenticity of the Ark and its whereabouts, hell I am not even Christian. I find good things and bad things in all religions, but I guess you could call me a "doubting Thomas. You remember that in your Catechism days, don't you?" She did not wait for a response, instead added, "Jesus said to Thomas, remember, doubting Thomas, when the Lord appeared to him, and told him to place his fingers in his wounds etc., and Thomas declined, saying he now believed." Frank said "yes."

"And Jesus said to him, blessed are those that believe, but have not seen." That always reminds me when I am in a doubting mode, to stop questioning. I know that sounds like a copout. And then there is the scientist in me that is fascinated every time something from the Bible is found to be factual. I mean, recently they found that the Shroud did contain a male who showed signs of being crucified and that the garment contains human blood. That the head cloth that supposedly draped the fact of Jesus, contains the same blood type and matches up to the face on the Shroud of Turin. This is all backed by science. So, knowing that, it makes it easier for me to accept those passages in the Old Testament as being maybe exaggerated, but basically based on fact. So, what do you think of my premise?" she asked.

"Beauty and brains, and she is all mine," Frank said.

"You always say the right things to make a girl blush." Nancy said, blowing him a kiss which he caught.

CHAPTER 21

Without requesting them to do so, the group got back in their earlier seats and Nancy begin. "Ok, so as I was saying, since the disappearance of the Ark of the Covenant there have been several claims about who might have possession of it and where it might be located.

In my research over the years concerning the Ark, as well as the Shroud of Turin and the Sudarium of Oviedo, we know exactly where two of them are: The Shroud is in the Church or Turin, Italy, and the Sudarium is in the town of Oviedo, in Northern Spain. We are not as lucky with the whereabouts of the Ark."

She then clicked on a slide showing Ethiopia and then another slide showing a town named Axum. "This is the town of Axum, Askum in Ethiopian, and it is in Northern Ethiopia. It is located 6,991' above sea level. The town has a population of approximately 60,000 people, but this does not count the Christians who conduct a pilgrimage to the site each day. They pray outside the walls of both the main church and the chapel where the Ark of the Covenant is supposed to be located. Some of them show up at day break, and remain until dark.

The Ethiopian Orthodox Church has claimed that the Ark of the Covenant, or as they call it, the Talbot, is housed in their town, in the chapel next the Church of Our Lady Mary of Zion. The original church (slide) is believed to have been built during the reign of Ezana, the first Christian ruler of the Kingdom of Axum during the 4th century. As you can see in this slide, the original church has been rebuilt many times since.

In my research, I found documents showing that this guy, Menelik I (slide) somehow had possession of the Ark of the Covenant and that he left a forgery behind in the Temple of Jerusalem. He was an Abyssian and wrote in a document the following: (slide) "The Abyssinians possess also the Ark of the Covenant," and then he goes on with a description of the Ark. Another document I found disrupts this account, but indicates that after a stay of a few years in Egypt, the Ark did in fact, end up in Axum.

Let's fast forward to June 25, 2009 in which the patriarch of the Orthodox Church in Ethiopia announced that the next day, June 26, 2009, there would be an unveiling of the Ark to the entire world."

Everyone in the group apart from Frank, leaned a little bit forward in anticipation of Nancy's next slide, but there was none. Instead she motioned to Frank who walked up in front of the others, while Nancy went and occupied where Frank had been standing.

Ed gazed with his lustful eyes, following Nancy's walk to Frank's prior position. Damn, Frank is so lucky, he thought.

Frank began, "The patriarch announced the next day, that he had changed his mind and would not unveil the Ark, but that he personally could attest to it."

"What an asshole. Who the hell made him God?" Ed said.

"What a bunch of shit. You have most of the world waiting in anticipation that they will get to see the Ark of the Covenant, and this jerk, on his own, decides to play a game of bait and switch." Joe was really hot when he said this, even though it had occurred back on 2009.

Frank waited for the commotion to stop and then he continued. "Reportedly, the Ark was moved to the Chapel of the Tablet which is located next to the old church because a divine 'heat' from the Tablets had cracked the stones of its previous sanctum."

"A what?" asked James.

"I will come back to that James. Let me go on." Frank said. "As Nancy said, the Ark of the Covenant is claimed to have been brought to Ethiopia by Menelik I after he visited his father King Solomon.

A guardian monk is appointed for life by the former monk before he dies. Only the guardian monk may view the Ark, in accordance with the Biblical accounts of the dangers of doing so for a non-priest or cleric. If the incumbent guardian dies without naming a successor, then the monks of the monastery hold an election to select the new guardian priest. The priest or monk, or whatever you want to call him, then is confined to the chapel of the Ark of the Covenant for the rest of his life, praying before it and offering incense.

Frank advances the next slide. "This gentlemen, is where we believe that Ark of the Covenant is located, in this small church or chapel. As you can see, it is enclosed by wrought iron fencing with curved spikes as the top.

I am guessing from this picture Nancy took of the guardian monk being visited by someone, that the fencing is about 8 feet tall. When I got next to it, that height was confirmed. By the way, it is very rare to see the guardian outside.

The group leaned forward to get a better look at the guardian, with Ruben and Joe, approaching the screen.

Ruben said, "He is not very short, is he? I had this idea that he would be short and bent over."

"No," Frank said, "he is about average height." "As I was saying, the fencing is not electrified.

Each section of fencing is attached to a metal pole cemented into the ground. The sections are bolted into an L-shaped bracket that is welded to the pole. More about that later.

Nancy and I walked around the perimeter taking pictures of the church and the chapel, with more concentration on the chapel. I estimate it to be about 40 feet by 50 feet, almost square. There are only a few volunteer guards around the outside. On the day we were there, we counted four max, but they were carrying AK-47s. They do not seem to have a protocol for regarding how they patrol the grounds. Sometimes they start to walk, see another guard, and stand together bull-shitting and sharing a smoke. Other times, they walk all the way around both the main church and the chapel. The only time their actions seem to be predictable, is when it is raining. They seem to prefer to stay indoors until the storm passes. We will use their standard operating procedure of staying out of the rain for our benefit when we hit the chapel. Thus, why we want to hit the place during the rainy season.

The walls of the chapel appear to be made of cinder block. If it is like any of the construction going on that we observed, they do not use re-enforced iron when they lay each new brick. They just slap on some mortar and keep on moving. We could not tell what the roof is made of. We know they had a bad leak back in 2011 and it had to be repaired, but beyond that, nothing. Taking all of this in consideration, I do not think that the cinder block construction or the fencing will be an issue for what I have planned.

Ed held up his hand like he was in school. Frank saw him and nodded. Ed said, “How does the guardian monk get his food?”

"What we saw was that this guy rarely comes outside, and when he does, it is either to meet someone at the gate or to take a stroll around the chapel. Again, he, like the guards, does not have a normal routine. Therefore, we surmise that he must have a kitchen, a refrigeration unit, and something to cook his meals, along with a fresh water supply and toilet. As you see in this slide, we see some worshippers come to the gate and leave a basket of food items for him. Generally, the items are left and he comes out later to get it. Again, it is rare that you see this." Frank was pointing to the guardian having interactions with pilgrims at the fence. "Since he will be in there until he is about to die, he is self- sufficient." Frank stopped and drank some coffee.

"On our last trip to Axum, Nancy and I tried to see if we could meet the guardian to help Nancy regarding her research, our cover story, and for me to gather more intel. We went to the office of Aksum's high priest, who works out of a tin shed at a seminary close by the Ark chapel. We thought that since he is the administrator in Aksum, he would be able to tell us more about the guardian of the Ark," Frank said.

"Wait a minute," Joe said. "You mean you two have already been there?"

"Four times," Frank said. "We have made a point of being seen there as much as possible on each trip, to solidify our cover story of Nancy, a well-known Biblical historian and Archeologist, studying the church, chapel, and the townspeople, for a future book. Frank looked at Nancy to see if she wanted to add anything. She did not add anything on.

Frank started again, "The high priest told us that the guardian prays constantly by the Ark, both day and night, burning incense before it and paying tribute to God. As I said, only the guardian can see it; all others are forbidden to lay eyes on it or even go close to it," Frank paused for effect since he knew he would later talk about supposed curses associated with those deemed unworthy who attempted to possess the Ark. "Over the centuries many people from the West who have come to Axum, claimed that they had seen and described it like those described in the Book of Exodus; you know, like the pictures Nancy showed you. But the Ethiopians say that is inconceivable—the visitors must have been shown fakes.

Even though Nancy and I knew through her research, how the guardian is chosen, we asked him, hoping to really establish a relationship before we hit him with the big question. He told us that the guardian was chosen by Aksum's senior priests and the present guardian. We acted as if this was new information for Nancy's research.

We thought that we had buttered the old guy up, so Nancy, in her flirtatious best voice, asked him if we could meet the guardian of the Ark. Talk about a total change in personality. The high priest stood even more upright and threw out his chest and said emphatically

"No, he is usually not accessible to ordinary people, just religious leaders."

"Not to give up so easily, Nancy suggested that we try again the next day. We hung around the outside of our hotel watching the pilgrims come and go to both the church and chapel. We saw a young priest near the gate of the Ark chapel. He seemed friendly in all of his contacts with those near the fencing, so we decided to hit him up.

This time, Nancy, after explaining who she was and why we were in Axum, asked him the same question I asked the big shot the day before. Instead of a repeat performance like we got from the senior monk, the young priest bowed, indicating that he understood Nancy's request.

To our surprise and with a smile, he said, "Wait here." He opened the gate, then climbed the steps leading to the chapel entrance where he called out softly to the guardian.

A few minutes later, he returned to where Nancy and I were standing with a big smile on his face. He turned towards the chapel and pointed. Soon we saw the monk, coming from the inside of the building, making a turn around the left wall, and upon seeing us, he began walking up to the fence which separated us from the courtyard area. He looked to be in his late 50s.

"It's the guardian," the priest whispered, acting kind of excited.

The guardian wore a robe medium green in color. He also wore a dark pillbox turban and sandals. He first glanced at Nancy and then warily at me with deep-set eyes. He held in his right hand a wooden cross that he stretched through the bars, towards Nancy. The wooden cross was painted yellow.

The priest who had contacted the guardian, motioned that we should box and let the guardian touch our foreheads, so that we could receive a blessing. The priest also mimicked that we should kiss the top and bottom of the cross, which we learned later, was the traditional way. Both Nancy and I did as instructed.

That completed, I asked the guardian for his name.

He still looked at me warily and responded in Ethiopian, saying, "I'm the guardian of the Ark." The priest translated that the guardian also further stated, "I have no one name."

Nancy, realizing what a once in a life time opportunity this was, told the younger priest to tell the guardian that we had come from the other side of the world to speak with him about the Ark of the Covenant.

The priest, continuing to act as our interpreter gave Nancy's request to the guardian who began shaking his head from side to side, followed by what the priest said was, "I can't tell you anything about it. No king or patriarch or bishop or ruler can ever see it, only me. This has been our tradition since Menelik brought the Ark here more than 3,000 years ago."

"He continued to peer at us, but mostly at me," Frank said. "I started to get a weird feeling, like he could read what was on my mind, and of course, that would be how to break into his chapel and steal the Ark."

Everyone in the room, including Nancy, laughed. "I tried to ask a few more questions, which our priest translated and directed to the guardian, but to each he remained as silent as an apparition. He continued to stare at me more than Nancy. Then, still silent, he turned, and walked back to the chapel. He was gone."

None of Frank's crew said anything. A few sipped their beer or drink.

Frank continued by saying that after the guardian left, he and Nancy turned towards the young priest, who must have read on our faces, our unspoken questions of what happened, why did he just leave?

"You're lucky, because he refuses most requests to see him," the priest said.

Frank said, "Nancy and I really didn't feel lucky, because I wanted to gain more intel. I mean, I wanted to know the layout of the chapel, especially where the Ark is located. I wanted to know if the Ark looks the way Nancy described it and see if he would have confirmed anything about how much gold is on the Ark; how much it weighed." Frank stopped speaking. "I would have asked the guardian if he has ever seen any sign of its awesome power?" said James, apparently still hung up on what he saw in the Indiana Jones' movie.

"Since he did not answer any other questions that day, we don't have a lot of answers, including a question like yours James. I thought about trying to get over the fence and slip inside using the darkness as cover, you know, to peer into a window for a look, but I believe that the guardian was a lot nimbler that he lets on, and would have caught me and set off any alarm he may have. And, before you ask James, no I was not held back by fear that the Ark would harm me if I dared defile it with my presence," Frank said with a grin on his face.

This time everyone laughed or chucked except James, who blushed, as noted by Nancy.

"So, with all this said, I can't be 100% sure that the Ark of the Covenant truly rests inside this nondescript chapel. But, when I add up all the information gleaned by Nancy in her years of research, the feeling I get when I am close to the Christians worshiping near the chapel, the traditions that the Ethiopians have followed for hundreds of years regarding their supposed possession of the Ark, and our brief encounter with the guardian, well, if I was a betting man, and I am, my money is on Nancy." With that he stopped and waited for any comments or questions. Receiving neither, he had them turn their attention back to the television screen.

"This slide is of the Middle East, in case any of you forgot. Remember the good times we had there? Frank asked. "Sorry James, not you."

And here is Axum." Frank pointed at the town. "Gee, the Ark of the Covenant is supposed to be in that shit-hole part of world? Lets' see, we have Somali, Yemen, Sudan and there is Ethiopia," an exasperated Jessie said.

"Yes, sorry Jessie, we think the Ark is in this part of the World. Next time, I will try to find a job in the Caribbean just for you."

"All right then, now we're talking," said Jessie. "Ok, now here is the plan I came up with that I want to run past all of you," said Frank. He continued, "Each of you, has a key part in the operation. But, first I must warn you of some consequences", Frank said, and he looked at Nancy.

The group of men, followed his eyes and gazed on the only woman present, to see if from her body language, they could learn in advance what Frank was about to reveal. No luck.

Frank continued, "I have known all of you including James, for at least 20 plus years. I also know that some of you are only "religious" when all hell broke loose on the battle field. You know that I am one of those that goes to Church sometimes, you know, Christmas and Easter, which might be a little oxymoron since I am a thief." Laughter filled the room.

"Also, like many of you, I have pretty much violated each of the Ten Commandments and it surprises me each time I walk into church that it doesn't come crashing down on me." Frank took a pause.

"But do you have a bad case of hemorrhoids Frank?" asked Ruben jokingly.

"No, Ruben, and thank you for asking you asshole," Frank responded.

"Aside from the fact that we are going to be operating in a sovereign nation, I need to be totally upfront with you about the dangers, seen and possibly unseen, that we might encounter," he said. He then paused and said, "You know, Nancy, actually you are a lot more knowledgeable about this stuff, so guys, change of plan, why don't you take over?" With that all eyes turned back to Nancy again.

Getting back up in front of the group, Nancy, without using the Mac or the television screen, says, "Ok, I have to refer to some interpretations of biblical writings so that I can get to what Frank wants everyone to understand. First, God commanded Moses to put in the Ark three items: a golden pot of manna, Aaron's staff, and the two stone tablets on which the Ten Commandments were written. I don't remember if I defined what manna was before, but it was a type of food that God provided the Hebrews during their travels in the desert some 40 years or so. The cover is supposed to have be hammered out of solid gold including the cherubim.

"Yeah, that's what I'm talking about! Solid Gold, at today's prices, cha-ching!" shouted Joe.

Nancy smiled and went on, "God told Moses, tell your brother Aaron not to come whenever he chooses into the Most Holy Place behind the curtain in front of the atonement cover on the Ark, or else he will die, because God appeared in the cloud over the atonement cover."

"What a minute Nancy, if you don't mind," said James. "Maybe I am still using the Indiana Jones, Raiders of the Lost Ark movie as my reference point, but do you have an educated guess as to why those particular items were placed in the chest? I mean, aside from the gold lid or whatever you call it, it sure doesn't seem like God instructed anything of value to be placed inside?"

"Actually, James, that is a great question and one I ponder with both during my undergrad and graduate level research. I think that maybe if I went over what some ancient writings suggest, it will help the group understand the possible unseen dangers Frank started to talk about before he asked me to jump in again." She again opened her Mac and filled the television screen with a picture of an artist's rendition of manna. Nancy said, "James is correct, and many scholars have wondered the same question. That is, why, hidden in the special golden box representing God's presence, were not treasures and precious gems placed, but instead, three unlikely items: a jar of bread (manna), a stick (Aaron's rod) and two stones (the Ten Commandments). Why? Why would God give instructions to Moses, to put these unlikely items in the Ark?" Nancy paused.

"First, regarding manna, according to biblical texts, God said to Moses to put manna into the Ark so that generations to come could see the bread that God gave the Hebrews to eat in the desert when he brought them out of Egypt." Again, she paused, glanced at Frank for no reason and never referred to the citation (Exodus 16:32) that was at the bottom of the screen.

"Second, Aaron's staff that had budded. The Hebrews, out of jealousy, rebelled against Aaron as being their high priest. God got angry and commanded the people to take 12 sticks written with the names of the leader of each tribe and place them before the Ark overnight. To their amazement, the next day, Aaron's rod from the house of Levi, had budded with blossoms and almonds. God confirmed his choice of Aaron's household as the priestly line.

Nancy advanced to the next slide and read, "And the Lord said to Moses, 'Put back the staff of Aaron before the testimony, to be kept as a sign for the rebels, that you may make an end of their grumblings against me, lest they die.'" Again, she did not refer to the citation (Numbers 17:10).

She went on saying, "The staff reminded the Israelites that on more than one occasion, they had rejected God's authority.

"Third," Nancy continued, "the two stone tablets with the Ten Commandments: God had chosen the Israelites as His special people. For the Israelites to qualify for that distinction, God had demanded one thing.

They must obey His Law, the Ten Commandments. This was a conditional agreement: "Now if you obey me fully and keep my covenant, then out of all nations you will be my treasured possession. Although the whole earth is mine, you will be for me a kingdom of priests and a holy nation." (Exodus 19:5-6)." Nancy stopped and then said, "here comes the warnings about trying to possess the Ark of the Covenant."

Nancy went on while Ed was thinking to himself, that if his Bible teacher looked like Nancy, he probably would have been much more attentive.

Nancy said, "Well, the Israelites promised God that they would do all that he asked of them, you know, follow the Ten Commandments etc., but they did not fulfill their end of the contract and God is pissed to say the least. I mean, repeatedly, they violated God's holy Law, and God made it clear to them the consequences of their sin by sending plagues, natural hazards and foreign armies upon them. The stone tablets in the Ark were a reminder that the Israelites had rejected God's right standard of living."

"What do you mean plagues, natural hazards etc.?" Joe asked.

His question surprised Nancy, since he was so quiet when she first started her presentation earlier that morning. But, she thought, at least he is listening.

"Ok," Nancy said, looking at Joe. "One of the first references about the power of the Ark, takes place when, after the Philistines defeated the Israelites in battle and captured the Ark of the Covenant. What is interesting about this is that the Bible does not tell us about the destruction of one of the most important shrines of old Israel. The Ark was captured and the glory was gone from Israel.

The Ark narrative in the Bible tells us that God is not a slave to humankind; nor is he bound to human expectations. In the battle between the Israelites and Philistine armies, it was assumed by the Israelites that whoever controlled the Ark controlled God. They confused the symbol of God's presence with God himself, and they assumed that when they manipulated sacred symbols, they were manipulating God.

They hoped to bless their war against the Philistines by invoking the name of God, just like people do today. Just because you call on Allah or sing God Bless America before killing innocent people, it does not mean that God approves of your violence."

The Philistine army won and the Ark was placed as a trophy of war in the Temple of Dagon in Ashdod. The name Dagon is associated with grain, and he was a fertility god. We don't know for sure what he looked like, but a misunderstanding of Hebrew led to the widespread belief that he was a fish-god.

The Ark was placed before the idol, Dagon, but the next day the priests of Dagon found their god on the ground paying homage to the ark. That must have been quite a surprise, but they did what any government bureaucrat would do. They set Dagon upright and pretended that nothing had happened. No doubt they had to suppress rumors that there had been an incident in the Temple and resisted calls for an official inquiry into the falling of Dagon. Their attempt to pretend that all was normal was doomed to fail, though. Things just got worse.

The next day when they went into the temple, they probably brought along ropes and pulleys just in case he had fallen again, but this time they found that Dagon's head and hands had been removed from his body. This was a dramatic statement of anti-Dagonism. By removing the hands and head of the idol, the perpetrator had made the statement that the idol could neither act nor think. Dagon, the lord of the harvest and fruitfulness in Philistia was nothing more than a statue made by human beings.

What came next is clearly identified as the work of a God who was angry that his Ark was being kept in a pagan temple. A plague stalked the land. Along with the plague there was an infestation of rats that ravaged the crops. Dagon, the Lord of the harvest, was powerless to stop the rats. He had no hands or head.

There are some variations in copies of the Hebrew text, and it is not clear exactly what kind of plague struck the Philistines. The people had tumors or boils of some type. Some versions of the story specify that the boils were in a particularly painful and embarrassing area of the body, which one translator rendered as the "hinder parts," she stopped.

"Ouch!" said Ed, grabbing his crotch. Nancy laughed, but out of the corner of her eye, she could see that Frank wanted things wrapped up.

"Many historians suspect that the plague was actually the bubonic plague. The fact that the plague was accompanied by an infestation of rats supports that theory. Also, the statement that the plague spread from Philistine city to city from the coast to the inland as the Ark was relocated is consistent with bubonic plague. All types of plague are terrible, but the bubonic plague is one of the worst.

Called the Black Death in the Middle Ages, it wiped out nearly 1/3 of the population of Europe in just two years (1348-1350). Throughout history it has ravaged cities along trading routes, often during great prosperity. Plague was this mysterious force that struck like the Grim Reaper, cutting down rich and poor, good and evil without pity.

The priest had probably figured that since the trouble started when the Ark had been captured and Dagon had been decapitated, it made sense that the Ark was the cause of the plague. By taking the Ark into their temple, they had opened themselves up to the power of a god they did not worship or serve. Instead of being blessed by this symbol of God, they were cursed by it. There is a warning here for all people who call or invoke the name of God and symbols of religion. Do not expect a blessing from a God you do not worship and obey." Nancy paused before continuing.

"In a way, the story of the Ark's return is a micro-version of the story of the Exodus. God sends a plague and the enemies of Israel are forced to let the Ark return to Canaan. The Israelites did not send in an assault to bring the Ark out of Ekron, nor did they keep killing civilians until the Philistines relented.

It was God who acted, and the Philistines wisely consented. The Philistines made a connection between their plague and the story of the Exodus. It is not clear how they would have known that the LORD God had sent ten plagues on Egypt, but the Philistine priests told the rulers that they should learn from history. Don't harden your hearts the way Pharaoh did. Don't play around with fire. Give the Ark back as fast as you can, but they were not going to call the Israelites to come get their ark because that would be admitting defeat. They created golden rats in the same method as used by for the construction of the lid of the Ark and placed it inside, at least that is how the story goes."

Nancy takes a deep breath but is happy as she looks at everyone, she still had their attention. She continued, "With great caution and limited fanfare, the Ark was prepared for the return to Israel. New milk cows would return the Ark for them. The tension in the biblical story involves what the cows will do. The cows had just calved. If they turned back to their calves, then the Ark was not the problem. If they went straight down the road, then the Ark was the cause of the plague. This adds to the supernatural aspect of the story. Unguided, the cows unnaturally turn away from their mooing calves and journeyed down the road out of Philistia all the way to Bethshemesh.

The people of Bethshemesh were harvesting their crops when the Ark appeared. This was a subtle reminder that Dagon was not really the Lord of the harvest. The Israelites had a harvest without Dagon.

The people left their crops and followed the Ark to see where it would stop. It came to a large stone in the middle of a field. Clearly, this was one of the sacred stones in Canaan, like those mentioned in Genesis. The people used the wood of the cart to make a fire and then sacrificed the cows on the altar stone in the field. The priests of Israel also placed the golden offerings on the stone for God. The five lords of the Philistines watched all this and reported it back in Ekron where they probably sacrificed the calves. With a little humility, these leaders had saved their cities.

"I could go on, but Frank is giving me the evil eye." Nancy said.

"Never mind about Frank, Nancy," said Jessie. "Go ahead and finish the story."

Looking at Frank, who was returning to the fireplace area with another cup of coffee, she saw him start to laugh, once again noticing what a great lecturer she is, totally captivating his Banshees.

"The story continues to an uncomfortable ending. Some of the people did not join in the festivities. They may have even desecrated the Ark by looking inside it. The texts are ambiguous. Whatever their offense was, the Lord killed seventy of them, or perhaps as many as 50,000 according to some texts. In other words, the plague was carried into Israel itself and there was great grief. The return of the Ark was not a universally good thing, and the people of that region wanted to be relieved of the burden of caring for such a dangerous item. They sent word to another village that the Ark had been returned and they should get it. Oddly enough, they failed to mention that people were dropping like flies – or fleas.

So, the Ark finally came to rest in the home of Abinadab on a hill, and the plague finally ran its course. No explanation is given for why the Ark was not sent to one of the shrines of Israel. Perhaps none of the other priests wanted to take the chance, but Abinadab was willing. His son, Eleazar, was consecrated to care for the Ark.

What can we make of this grim and somber ending of the story of the Ark? This is one of those stories that make many people uncomfortable with the Old Testament." She looked at Frank and remembered their earlier talk after their passionate engagement.

"There is so much death and violence, some of it senseless. The death of those who did not rejoice seems like a random act of violence, like the shootings on a college campus. Whether it was 70 or 50,000 does not lessen the problem. One way to deal with this is to explain it away scientifically and point out that plague rats probably followed the Ark. Like all epidemics, this one ended eventually on its own.

Another way is to deal with the story theologically.

"What do you mean Nancy, theologically?" asked James.

Nancy responds, "Well, from my point of view, it is a stark reminder that God is not Santa Claus. Though we try to domesticate God, he is beyond our categories of good and evil, kind or cruel. The experience of God as holy is to experience God as dangerous as well as good. Sorry for my preaching but I want to say a little more.

The third way to deal with this story is the most popular. We simply keep it out of the lectionary so we don't have to preach about it on Sunday mornings." Everyone, including Frank, laughed.

"This is a strange and compelling story about the sovereignty and power of God. The Bible does not interpret this story for us, but it leaves us to make sense of it if we can. I think that the most important point that people of faith can take from this story today is that God is not our property. We cannot build a gilded chest in which we lock up his power to bless and curse. We cannot carry God into battle to slay or enemies or set him up a Temple as a trophy. We need to respect the mystery of God, and pray that we are doing his will. God can fight his own battles; we do not have to engage in holy wars."

The first person to speak was Frank who said, "This is a good time to take a long overdue break, let's grab some lunch that I have spread out on the kitchen table, get a beer or drink, hit the head, and then I will discuss the plan."

Everyone got up, some stretched. Nancy walked up to Frank and said, "What do you think, babe?"

"Hey, you kept every one's attention, including mine," Frank responded. "Good job, now it is up to me."

CHAPTER 22

"Alright guys, listen up," Frank started off. "I held off until lunch, before having Nancy explain some of the biblical documentations about the consequences to those deemed unworthy, coming in contact with the Ark. Whether you believe or disbelieve, or chalk- up boils, plague, death etc. to superstition or just nonsense, I felt you needed to know."

"Bunch of bullshit is what I think," said Ruben.
"Me too," said Ed.

"Frank, you had us come here to present to us with a plan and see if we are interested. Don't you think it is about time.?" Jessie said.

All eyes were now on Frank, not Nancy. "First," Frank said, "does anyone want out?"

Frank looked around the room. The only one who seemed a little uncomfortable was James.

Sensing that, Frank called on him. "What about it James? Are you in?"

James hesitated and then said, "Hell yes, I am in."

"That's the way to grow a bigger set of balls," said Ed. Everyone except Frank laughed.

"First, since this will be our biggest heist yet, you can expect a lot of planning, dry runs, everything like we did before a major black-ops. In addition, each of you must get a visa for Saudi Arabia, Ethiopia and Eritrea, so you might get started on that asap. You can order one through the Ethiopian embassy here in the states, or when you arrive at the airport. At the airport, it costs $50 U.S. dollars. Nancy, who is better at researching the Web, will email you some sites you can use that will expedite your visa requests for Saudi Arabia and Eritrea.

Having said that, Frank said, almost as an afterthought, "actually you guys, I would like each of you to apply for a visa one month apart. Not at the airport. You, therefore, will need three visas, one for Saudi Arabia, one for Ethiopia and one for Eritrea. James, you will apply for your visas as soon as possible since you will be the first part of the operation. More about that later. Next month, Joe, then Jessie, then Ruben, and finally you Ed. We do not want to create activity that looks suspicious, and I think it would, if someone was watching us, and saw five Americans, all applying for a Saudi, Eritrea and Ethiopian visa at the same time."

Pointing to Nancy, he said, "Nancy and I already have secured our visas so we are set. She and I, as I said, have traveled to Axum four times already and made sure that many people there saw us so our reappearance in the future should not set off any alarms.

"What do the locals think the two of you are there for?" asked Joe.

"Well, like I said before, since Nancy is all over the Internet being a professor and all, our cover is that she is researching the Ark of the Covenant as well and the locals. This way, if someone is suspicious, when they conduct a Google search, it is verified that she is an academic," Frank responded.

"What about you?" Joe asked.

"They can Google me all they want and will not find anything," Frank said, "but if they go to Facebook and type in Nancy's name, there are several placed pictures of her and I as lovers visiting several different holy sites. That should satisfy anyone."

"I have planned for our raid to take place about one year from today. That will give us plenty of time to make travel arrangements, gear purchases and establish connections and do a few dry runs. We will execute the raid in either July or August since that actually is when the heaviest rainfall occurs."

"Why are we doing it in the rainy season?" asked Ed.

"One, we are hoping that the heavy rain will damper any noise we may make. Secondly, I told you that on the four occasions Nancy and I have been there, we have seen young armed volunteers that sporadically walk near the chapel. We never saw more than four at a time, but we do not know for sure. When it did rain however, they did not like to go outside. I think that is the best time to execute the plan."

Nancy brought a beer for everyone including Frank. "Thank you," he said, and then he continued. Using the Mac, Frank showed the chapel again, as well as a hotel across the street. "Nancy will be our spotter and will be located in the top floor of this hotel overlooking the whole operation. We stayed there on the other four trips so no one should be the wiser. We will all use the same communication devices we used in our past adventures and Nancy can keep us appraised of any problems.

Back to you James. Since you almost earned your private yacht license, I feel you are the best prepared to be the captain of the yacht. You four, (pointing to Ed, Jessie, Ruben and Joe) will be using it for you approach from Saudi Arabia up into the Red Sea to the coastline of Eritrea.

Frank went back to the slide showing the area, and using a laser pointer, showed James and the others, the sea route they would be using.

"Once you get your visas, you will fly to Riyadh where you will be contacted by some individuals who are helping to "sponsor" this event. From Riyadh, they will take you to Jeddah which is on the West coast of Saudi Arabia near Mecca. There they will take you to the yacht and introduce you to a hand-picked crew that will be assisting you. Later, you will receive a few ladies that will be traveling with you; helping you act out your cover story of a wealthy American playboy.

"Lucky you, kid," said Jessie.

"Yeah, but will he know what to do with them?" asked Ed, sounding a little jealous that this was not his assigned task. Everyone else laughed, while James blushed.

"Everyone you will meet James, are highly reliable, even the ladies, and no, not in the way you are thinking Ed," Frank said. They do not know what the plan is, but they are aware that they will be extremely well paid if they do whatever is requested of them, including keeping their silence.

"Your crew, James, will bring the material and supplies we will need for the job. I will cover the equipment later, but by having our Saudi contacts bring the equipment, we avoid any problems trying to get things through the airport, customs etc. Once the equipment is stored onboard, we should be ok, since neither the Saudis or other countries in the area have anything resembling our U.S. Coast Guard to stop, board and inspect the yacht.

James, once you get to the marina, you will start partying at some of the clubs, flashing a lot of money with your ladies by your side. Some of the Muslim women will be upset about your activity and your lady companions, but believe me, the Muslim males will be jealous.

Staggered two days apart, Jessie, then Ed, followed by Joe and Ruben, will arrive by taxi to meet up with you at the marina. They will also be playing the part of wealthy Americans out for a good time.

Jessie retired from the NFL. Joe is a professional stunt man, and Ed is an investment banker. Ruben is real estate tycoon. You will all have Websites and Facebook accounts set up for you from our friends in the Middle East before we put the plan in action. If anyone wants to check, there is your cover. Read them so you know what they say about you. They should be up by the end of this month.

As I said, Nancy has already placed Internet and Facebook crap online about her and me.

James, you also have stuff about you on the Internet, so please read it before you leave on your trip," Frank paused to take a drink form the beer Nancy brought him.

"Frank, I have a question," asked Joe. "Go ahead," said Frank.

Joe continued, "I know you said that James' crew etc., will not know about our mission, but it sure sounds like this heist is going to cost a lot of cash before we even pull it off, and gee, when the plan is executed, you're talking visas, equipment, yacht, crew members, escorts. That said, who is bankrolling us?" Frank responded, "You are right Joe. To pull this off without sending off any red flags, will require tons of cash and support from individuals in the Middle

East. If I did not have their backing and bankroll, we would be dead in the water before we even started. That said, I have re-established our connections with those individuals who helped us out in our black ops assignments. I mean, those missions that we decided to pull without Uncle Sam or the Army knowing anything about it." Everyone except Nancy laughed.

Even though they were lovers, Frank never revealed to Nancy, his team's nefarious actions while they served their country. For her, that was no problem. She, too, had skeletons in her closet.

With the money and support of these individuals, we should go first cabin all the way; thus, solidifying our cover stories to the max. I think all of you will be impressed along the way. Does that answer your question Joe?" Frank asked.

"Sure did, thanks Frank."

"Ok, back to the mission plan," said Frank. "Nancy and I will set up shop in Axum several weeks, before the operation. While we are there, James will make his way to Saudi Arabia where he will pick up the yacht, crew members, and ladies of the night. He will party with the ladies both at the marina as well as setting out for a few excursions with the boat. I want you to be seen and heard.

Eventually the four of you will meet up with James and continue to party and generally make a scene wherever you are. I will contact James when I want the operation to commence. When the order to execute comes, James will slowly head in this direction up into the Red Sea. Using coordinates that I will send you, you will anchor somewhere off the coastline of Eritrea. You will wait for my signal at which time you four will take the speed boat, with your equipment, from the yacht and head for the beach, around this area pointing to the map again.

From the beach, you will climb up to a road about here. There you will find a large military type truck containing several ATVs. The keys to the truck and ATVs will be inside the cab. I will send you the coordinates as to where you are to drive. When you arrive at those coordinates, you will remove the ATVs and head to your second set of coordinates, where you will set up your base camp." Any questions so far?" Frank asked.

"Yeah Frank," James said. "What am I supposed to be doing while this is going on?"

"You will remain on the yacht until these guys, pull the job and return with the Ark," Frank replied. He continued, "I cannot precisely tell you how long you must wait, but hey, you will have all the ladies for yourself."

Again, one of the Banshees shouted out, "Yeah, but will you know what to do with them?" Frank could not tell who said it, but it got a lot of laughs.

Frank continued with the plan. "We are hoping for a large storm to hit the area and when that occurs, I will notify you four to advance on the chapel.

You will use the ATVs to get to this position, using another slide to show the rear of the chapel area. Use this cover to leave the ATVs. One of the ATVs, a Ranger model (no pun intended) will be used to transport the Ark.

Once Nancy gives you the all clear from her vantage point, you will move up to the rear fencing, here." Frank advances to a new slide. It is a close-up of a section of wrought iron fencing.

"Using a noise reduction grinder, one of you will hit these areas of the L-bracket and remove a section of the fence. Once removed, the four of you will enter and then replace the section of fencing, attaching it to the pole with good old duct tape, for a temporary period; just in case a guard decides to walk the perimeter."

Next slide, "You will decide which window pane to score. You will have in your equipment, a score tool, that after you make your cut, will allow the hose attached to the gas, to enter the chapel.

"We will be using a calmative to knock out the guardian," he said.

"What's a calmative?" James asked.

"Sorry James, these old warhorses already know, and I forgot you were not in the Armed Forces.

A calmative is a gas that is supposed to put a person asleep without being lethal," Frank said .

"Didn't the Russian use that when Chechen rebels seized more than 700 hostages in a Moscow theater several years ago? If I remember, it didn't work and instead over 100 hostages were killed." James responded.

"Hey look, the kid has brains and looks," Ed joked. He got a few laughs.

"You are spot on. The Russians took a lot of international heat for that screw up, but our own US military has become infatuated with a variety of "incapacitating" chemical weapons, including fentanyl, the opiate believed to have been used by the Russian, and believe that they now have a 100% non-lethal "calmative."

Not reported by our government, we used it during our black-ops several times and there have been no causalities. Whatever they did, they perfected it. It's called "Special K" and our Saudi contacts will bring the gas to the yacht. Once it arrives James, you and your crew need to hide it and secure it." Frank took another sip of beer.

"Oh, I forgot. I need to go back a little in my plan," Frank said.

"The four of you will continue to party on the yacht, go clubbing with James for a day or so, and then show everyone watching that you intend to go sport fishing. You will buy some fishing gear needed to fish for Grouper, Kingfish, Cobia, Queenfish, the local fish in the area," another pause and sip of beer by Frank.

"I will give you a call on a burner phone as to the date you need to set sail for Eritrea. I will give you plenty of sailing time so you do not have to push it.

Be prepared for any setbacks. If Nancy and I feel ANYTHING that might jeopardize our plan, we will pass it on to the four of you immediately. This is big, and we cannot screw up due to being impatient." Frank stopped and then said "Ok, that's enough for now, let's have some dinner and then we can finish up. I hope everyone likes spaghetti and meatballs."

CHAPTER 23

After everyone had enough spaghetti, meatballs, garlic bread, salad and wine, Frank started off again. "I'm getting old and can't remember where I left off, so if I repeat myself, deal with it. When the four of you arrive on the coastline of Eritrea, you will wait for my call as to when to start cross country into Ethiopia. In Eritrea, "friends" will have arranged for you to pick up some vehicles in which at night time you will transfer our supplies and gas. The equipment will consist of gas masks, night vision googles, our communication stuff, noise reduce grinder, cell phone jammer, wire cutters, camouflage. Let me go over the rest of the plan and if any of you think we need something else, let me know," Frank clicked to a new slide.

The slide showed a picture of the chapel. The front door was partially covered by two large pieces of cloth the entire length of the door. There appears to be a rod running horizontal across the threshold of the door, showing the two pieces of cloth pushed to two sides showing the large wooden door behind.

To the sides of the door, about three feet away, at the end of the cinder block walls are two large windows. They looked like stained glass, but it was hard to tell in the picture. The façade along the sides looked the same with the exception of having no entry door. The back, also had two windows and looked identical to the two sides.

"Ok, as you can see, it really looks like a perfectly square building. One way in and that is the only way out, unless, by chance, there is an underground passage way, and there is no way to find that out." Frank paused so that everyone could consider that for a moment.

On the night you hit the chapel, the following needs to be done;

One, someone will need to jam any cellphone activity and cut any telephone lines that Nancy and I were able to locate before you arrived.

Two, I only want to use explosives on the front door, so to get past the fencing, someone will cut the wrought iron fencing with the grinder, in such a way, that once you get inside the courtyard area, you can place it back in such a way that no one notices anything amiss.

Three, someone will use the Range-R to see if in fact, the guardian is the only one inside. That person will report back to everyone. "

"What is a Ranger-R." asked James.

"No, it's called a Range-R and both the military and police use the device to see if a suspect or suspects are in a room etc." said Frank.

"Hey, that's cool" said James.

"Four, after scoring a small hole of the glass window you insert a hose to deliver the gas. We will need a small rag or something to place around the hole just in case it is not a perfect fit.

Five, I will be in front of the hotel smoking a cigarette in contact with Nancy. If she sees anybody getting curious. I will take them out.

Six, after the gas is pumped into the chapel, we will wait 5 minutes and again, with the Range-R, see if we can detect any movement.

"How long does it take for the gas to work?" asked James, showing his lack of military experience.

"We have seen it work almost instantaneously, but we have heard from some of our colleagues that occasionally a person exposed to the gas, takes a little longer" Frank said.

"Seven, if no movement is noted inside, and this is the trickiest part, someone will have to go around to the front door and place the smallest amount of explosives on the hinges of the door. We only want to use enough to break the hinges, not demolish the door. Try to time the detonation to when the rain is really pouring.

Remember, we hope that anyone, especially those guards with their AK-47s, were to walk outside for a smoke, they would notice nothing out of the ordinary. "Once the door is breached, the four of you will go inside" Frank said. "You will find the Ark, and if no poles are present, use the telescopic poles in your equipment, to transport the Ark, out of the chapel to the ATVs. Once you have secured the package, you will notify me and Nancy, and wait until we check the area, to make sure that your retreat is clear. If the all clear is given, you will head out, while the trailing two, place the front door back as best you can so that any passerby's will not detect anything. Taking the ATVs, you will return to base camp, notifying me, once you arrive. If all goes as planned, you will backtrack all the way to the beach, and take the speed boat back to the yacht.

James, you and your crew will be gassed up and ready to set sail with your fellow filthy American buddies, when they arrive." Frank said.

James nodded and Frank continued. "Ok, that's the plan. Any questions, suggestions, or comments?'

"Once we get inside, what should we expect to find?" asked Ruben asked.

Frank looked at Nancy who took the cue that she needed to respond to Ruben's question.

"Ruben, I really don't know. There have never been postings of pictures of what it looks like inside; where the guardian lives, sleeps, eats, nothing. We don't even know where the Ark is kept. I wish I could give you guys more information, but it does not exist to my knowledge." With that, Nancy looked back at Frank. No one had any follow up questions, so Frank suggested that they all head into the kitchen and have some coffee and chocolate cake. He felt satisfied that to this point, the plan that he had drawn up was sound and had a good chance of success. But, his philosophy of preparing for the worst, so when it happens, you will not be surprised, constantly was in the back of his mind. In all his black ops gigs, he always played "what if " games in his head, in hopes of always having a plan B or even C.

CHAPTER 24

Rain was pouring down on the sidewalk near 950 Pennsylvania Avenue in Washington D.C. Agents Loomis, McCormick and Flores arrived at the U.S. Department of Justice only a few minutes late due to the rain for a meeting with their counterparts in Interpol. The building, named after the late Robert F. Kennedy looked similar to the old J. Edgar Hoover building that housed the Federal Bureau of Investigation, but, like that structure, now had various barricades in an attempt to make a terrorist attack on the building a lot harder. It appeared to have at least ten stories inside and Interpol was located on the 7th floor.

They all climbed out of the elevator and made their way to the solid oak door leading to their destination. Upon entering they were greeted by a young black receptionist who had been expecting them.

"Agent Loomis, correct?" she asked, looking at everyone but focusing on the female of the group of three.

"Yes," responded Loomis.

"Mr. Delaney is expecting you. Let me buzz him that you are here," the receptionist said as she picked up her phone.

"Sir, Agent Loomis and her team are here. Yes sir, I will let them know." The receptionist hung up her phone and with a smile said that Mr. Delaney will be here shortly."

Before any of them took a seat in the outer office where the receptionist was located, an interior door opened and into the room came a well- dressed male, approximately 6'2" tall with gray hair and a trimmed mustache. He immediately extended his hand to Agent Loomis and introduced himself. As they finished up their handshake, Loomis introduced Flores and McCormick. Handshakes continued and then Delaney opened the large oak door and ushered them in to a large conference room located to the right of a long hallway.

After entering the room, Delaney pointed to a table that had coffee, hot water, creamer, sugar and sugar substitutes, as well as a platter of sweet rolls. "Please, everyone, help yourselves to refreshments," he said. All the agents proceeded to the table and selected their beverage and food items. After helping themselves, they were once again directed by Delaney to an extremely large, highly polished, oak table that had twenty high-back style leather chairs with plush foam.

"Sure beats what we have in our office," said McCormick, directed towards no one in particular.

"You're right about that," said Flores.

"So, agent Loomis, from what you told me on the phone, something productive came about in the meeting up in a cabin in Idaho," asked Delaney.

Interpreting this as a time to start the official meeting, Loomis responded. "Yes, if fact we learned a lot about the overall plan and it execution. However, we still do not know the exact day nor the time they plan to execute. The only reference given by their ring leader is that they want to commit the raid during the rainy season in Ethiopia. That really doesn't narrow it down for us, and of course, our jurisdiction ends once they leave the soil of the U.S." "Yes, I understand, and of course, Interpol is prepared to take over all aspects of the investigation once it leaves the United States," Delaney responded. He added, "As you know, pop culture has been portraying our agency as a supranational law enforcement agency, but in fact, we have no agents who are able to make arrest. We primarily function as a network of criminal law enforcement agencies located throughout many different countries. We pass on what we have gained through our investigation network to the local and/or federal law enforcement agencies who actually make any arrests.

This investigation is a natural fit for your agency and ours as well as the federal police in Ethiopia.

Therefore, we will be operating as a liaison between all agencies involved." Saying this, Delaney looked at everyone in the room to make sure they were all on the same page. Not hearing any objections or questions, he went on.

While most agencies have extensive databases such as yours and the C.I.A., most end at a nation's borders. This is where Interpol's database can track criminals and crime trends around the world. We have the ability to collect and store fingerprints, face photos and recognition, DNA samples, track travel documents and attempt to locate wanted persons. Currently we have a database of more than 12 million records.

We have an encrypted Internet-based worldwide communications network which allows Interpol agents and member countries to contact each other at any time. We call it our I-24/7, and this network offers constant access to Interpol's databases. While the National Central Bureaus are the primary access sites to the network, some member countries have expanded it to key areas such as airports and border access points. Member countries can also access each other's criminal databases via the I-24/7 system. In fact, our office in Ethiopia is one of those countries." He stopped, feeling that he was dominating the meeting. The agents continued to focus on what Delaney was saying as well as consuming their brunch. Agent Loomis pretty much knew everything Delaney had said due to previous work with agents of Interpol, but for McCormick and Flores, this was great stuff.

Delaney continued, "Of course, all agencies are as good as, how do you say it in America, "its weakest link?"

"Yes, that is correct," said Loomis.

Delaney than said, "This James Hawkins I believe illustrates what I am referring too. He is obviously a weak link in U.S. Customs. We also have had our "weak links" with not only hackers trying to gain access to our databanks, but also the occasional dirty agent. So, with this in mind, I feel a strong need to keep our shared information on a need-to-know basis until we can wrap up our investigation. Agreed?"

All three agents showed signs of agreement.

CHAPTER 25

Delaney picked up a phone on the desk and requested that someone bring in the computer and projector for the room. He apologized to the agents that someone had forgotten to set up the conference room correctly. An extremely young male entered the room, followed by the receptionist they had first met in the outer office. Agent Loomis felt that the young male was probably an intern. He quickly set up the lap top and projector with the aid of the receptionist, and once completed, they both left the room. There was no conversation among anyone while they were present.

"This is what we have learned so far from our agents about your Banshees and their leader, Frank Silva, as well as this Dr. Nancy Harding.

(Slide advance- showing Frank Silva and Harding window shopping)

"First, I must inform you that trying to tail Silva is very difficult. It is almost as if he is paranoid. He constantly uses windows to mirror any suspected tail. When he drives, he runs through red lights to lose any possible surveillance. He has been extremely well trained. This photo was taken a few days ago in Riyadh. As you can see, they are posing as girlfriend/ boyfriend or is this relationship legit?" he asked.

"We believe that they are in fact, in a relationship from everything we have learned about them," replied Loomis.

Delaney nodded before he went on. "On this date, the two of them made contact with this individual, Khalid Abboud (slide advance showing a middle-aged male wearing a white thobe). Abboud is a very wealthy Saudi making his riches in the opium trade. Your C.I.A. should have a file on him since he is buying up a lot of your country such as Monterey, California and parts of Hawaii.

He and Silva stayed for almost a half hour at this outdoor coffee shop while Dr. Harding went shopping. We have no knowledge about what they discussed, but it appears that they reached some sort of agreement by shaking hands.

"Gee, even while shaking hands, he is surveying the area checking for tails," said McCormick.

"Yes, our agent was fortunate to find a shop across the street from the two of them with black out windows," replied Delaney.

(Slide advance) "This is Nadir Halabi, a flesh merchant. He is the worst form of a human. He has a network of kidnapping young females and auctioning them off to the highest bidder. Your agency may have a file on him no?" He looked at agent Loomis.

"I will have to check when I get back. Due to his international "trade," perhaps Homeland Security and the C.I.A. have something on him," she responded.

"You have not been able to bring him to justice Mr. Delaney?" asked McCormick.

"We thought we had him a few times, but our informants came up dead before trial," Delaney answered.

"Once again, we could not get close enough to hear the conversation, but we assume it had something to do with Halabi's business. How that fits into Frank and Dr. Harding's plan to steal the relic, we have no idea.

We followed them to the Riyadh airport where, before boarding their plane, they went into a restaurant to have a short lunch. Initially it looked harmless to our agent who took a seat at the bar and ordered a drink. Several tables away, an individual leaves his seat and walks over to Frank and Dr. Harding's table, carrying his drinking glass. Our agent did not know the identity of this person, who produced from a briefcase, what looked like brochures of All-Terrain-Vehicles. Frank examined the information in the documents and appeared to make some selections, after which, he shakes hands with the individual who leaves. Our agent waited until Frank and Dr. Harding left, at which time he picked up the drinking glass for later fingerprint analysis.

His name is Tamar Rassul, an Egyptian. We could find no criminal record on him, only that he seems to travel a lot from Egypt to Saudi Arabia. He lists himself as an import/export executive for a large power sports equipment, thus the ATV material he showed to Silva." Delaney motioned to everyone to again help themselves to refreshments as he too, refilled his coffee cup and grabbed another sweet roll. Agents Flores and McCormick did so, but Loomis remained at the table. Delaney returned to his seat and advance another slide but waited until Flores and McCormick were seated. "Silva and Dr. Harding next flew out to Axum International Airport where another agent picked up their arrival. As I said, we have a large office housed with the Federal Police Department in Ethiopia, so we had easy access to fresh agents which came in handy dealing with Frank's constant probing for surveillance. They checked into this hotel which is located across from the chapel. After checking in, they strolled down to this restaurant (picture shown) for an early dinner perhaps. On the surface, none of their activity seemed suspicious to our agents in the town, but they did spend a tremendous amount of time taking pictures of the chapel and its surroundings. After analysis, we believe that they were collecting intelligence.

Here our agent got a picture of them talking to the guardian of the chapel. Unknown what was discussed, but it did not last very long. They then walked back to their shared room at this hotel and stayed inside until the next morning. All total, they stayed in Axum for three days, returning on the third day. This concludes what we have found to date." With that, Delaney waited for any response from the group.

Agent Loomis asked Flores and McCormick if they had any questions which they did not.

"Thank you so much, Mr. Delaney. What you have shown us starts completing the puzzle we have about the plan and how they will try to execute it. For example, it appears from what you showed us, that they will be using ATVs to transport the Ark once it is secured. I have not figured out the involvement of those other two individuals, Abboud and Halabi, but I am sure that whatever they will contribute will go to the furtherance of the heist. So, for now, it appears we, both our agency and yours, will play a wait and see game pending more information as to when the operation goes into effect. I will contact you immediately once we learn that information so that your organization can take over. With this most recent trip to Axum by Silva and Harding I feel that the day is approaching when Frank will give his team the go."

Delaney agreed with Agent Loomis that he and his agency look forward to a joint investigation and offered that his agency in return, will forward any new information they obtain. Handshakes were exchanged and the agents left the conference room.

CHAPTER 26

On a sunny Saturday morning before her planned trip to Arizona with Frank, Nancy parked her Jeep in the faculty parking lot of the university and grabbed her briefcase, then attacked the numerous stairs up to the entrance of the history department. She had told Frank that she would not be able to be with him today because, with the end of the semester at hand, she needed to complete final grades as well as meet with doctoral candidates whom she advised regarding their dissertations. She waited until noon, figuring that if he had followed her, it was now verified that she was working this Saturday. Frank had not shown any signs that he suspected her of anything other than the love she had shown him.

She returned to her vehicle and began leaving the faculty parking lot, checking in her rearview mirror for any signs of Frank. She used some of the driving techniques she had seen Frank use to avoid anyone tailing her, with the exception of deliberately blowing red lights. By the time she reached the Interstate, she felt confident that Frank was not following her.

It took her almost 1 ½ hours to reach the little bed-and-breakfast inn secluded in the countryside. She seemed to always run late and this afternoon was no exception. She had stopped to use the restroom and grab a sandwich at a fast-food place, and even eating her burger while driving, still fell behind her intended arrival time. But, she thought, I will make it up to him and everything will be fine.

He had text her the room number of one of the bed-and-breakfast detached little cottages. She thought it looked so quaint. She grabbed her briefcase and overnight suitcase and walked to the door. Instead of knocking, she checked the door and found it open. While entering she said, "knock, knock, anyone here?"

Coming out of the bathroom, James showed signs of a recent shower and had a large size towel wrapped around his waist.

"Wow," said Nancy. "I think I definitely have the right place!"

"Come here you," said James. He wrapped his arms around Nancy's waist and pulled her tightly to him. She gave a soft moan along with a long passionate kiss, but as his hands begin to roam, she pulled away and said that she needed to jump in the shower due to the long drive.

James gave a brief but hallow objection and followed Nancy with his eyes and she took her overnight bag and disappeared behind a closing bathroom door. James turned on the television set and found a stage that was dedicated to playing the latest top 100 popular songs. He knew that Nancy shared the same type of music he had selected since both shared the same generation.

Through the music he could hear the shower run and he began to fantasizing about what would be taking place in this small cottage bedroom soon. He felt himself getting excited, so he decided to drop the towel and get into bed. He heard the shower stop and after a moment, a hair dryer start up. Any moment now he thought.

What seemed to him as an eternity, the dryer stopped and the door opened. Steam was the first to exit, followed by Nancy totally nude. She had taken the time to not only dry her hair, but arrange it the way James loved. He could also detect the perfume he and she had picked out together when they first met prior to their first intimate encounter.

Nancy did not speak but instead let her eyes do the talking. She approached the bed and James lifted the sheets from her side. Not wasting time, Nancy slid over to James and placed her left leg over his groin, detecting his hardness.

"What do we have here?" she asked coyly.

"I don't know" he said, "but I think they have snakes up here so maybe you should check it out."

Nancy giggled as she removed her leg from his groin and replaced it with her left hand, stroking him ever so gently. "God, you feel good, babe," she said as she kissed him, inserting her tongue into his waiting mouth.

James responded by brushing the back of his hand over Nancy's raising nipples. He then used his other hand to run his fingers through her hair which seemed to get Nancy even more excited.

Trying to stop a premature climax, James forcibly grabbed Nancy and threw her onto her back, pinning her arms over her head. He kissed her deeply, playing tongue tag with her. He released one hand but she kept it there as if still restrained. He lowered his head to her breasts and began softly licking and then sucking their nipples. Nancy began turning her head side to side in pleasure.

Finally, when they both felt that each of them were ready to climax, Nancy rolled on top of James and inserted him inside her very slowly to relish all the sensations that went with it.

Both exploded into each other as they were one, with Nancy continued to smash into James groin well after he had delivered, climaxing and climaxing again until the bottom sheet was wet with satisfaction shared by both.

CHAPTER 27

Nancy rolled off James and laid on her back while James reached to the adjacent nightstand and removed a cigarette from its pack. Nancy hated that James smoked, but tolerated it. After he lit the cigarette, he took a deep drag, but out of courtesy to Nancy, exhaled to the far side of the bed way from her.

Both knew that there was an elephant in the room, and Nancy was the first to bring it up. "That was so nice. Made the trip up here so worthwhile." James did not response so Nancy continued. "I know we talked about this before, but are you still ok, you know, with me and Frank?"

James at first, did not respond but instead took another drag on the cigarette. He turned towards Nancy after exhausting the smoke from his lungs, and said, "Look, we know what we both want and to get it, we have to do what has to be done right?" Before she could answer he went on. "Does it bother me that Frank makes love to you just like I just did?

Hell yes, and it is always uncomfortable seeing the two of you together and playing that we do not know each other."

Nancy jumped in and said, "First, no one makes love to me like you do. When I am with Frank, you must believe me that I am constantly thinking of you. But, as you said, we both want the same thing, and using Frank and his men, is the only way you and I can achieve it. In history, I always seem to bring up in many of my lectures, the word fate. Sometimes we run into good fate, and other times, bad fate.

You can use karma if you want, but think about it. You and I meet. I fall in love with you. I tell you about my research and how I believe I have located the exact location of the Ark of the Covenant. But, what can you and I do by ourselves? Nothing. You can call that bad fate. Then you meet Ed, and he in turn introduces you to Frank and his team of Banshees." When Nancy said Banshees she sarcastically put her two hands up to make quote marks.

James knew that Nancy strongly disliked Frank's former elite soldiers, classifying them as uneducated drunks and murderers who disgraced the uniforms they had worn, when she compared them to her late father, a former Marine, who died a few years ago.

"So now you and I gained good fate, since we now had a possible way to steal the Ark. All we had to do was formulate a plan to enlist Frank and his team and if fate continues on our side, we will secede in reaching our goal, and grow very old together." She waited to see if James would respond.

"You are right. This could not have worked out any better. I mean, what would the odds be that I would run into Ed at the gym and learn that he was part of an elite Black Ops squad and later be introduced to Frank. I think Frank initially did not trust me until I proved myself during my first bank job. He's never told you about any of our jobs, huh?" asked James.

"No, as you know, Frank is very private, even to me, and has never told me about any of the jobs you guys have pulled, nor what went on with his team in the war." Nancy said.

"I tell you though, Frank still scares me. At times, it seems like he sees right through people. Have you ever gotten that feeling?" James asks.

"Thank God no. I shudder to think what he would do if he found out about our plan or about us. I am hoping that he will continue to think that I am heads-over-heels about him so that he continues to trust me and indirectly, take pressure from you I hope," Nancy said as she began rubbing her fingers over James chest. Unlike Frank, James shaves his chest as smooth as a baby's bottom she thought.

"So, when do you two leave for Arizona?" James asked.

"I don't really know. Frank keeps his cards close to his chest and does not share much details with me. Most of the time I get a day's notice at best and he expects me to be ready to move. Once I learn anything I will let you know. How about you, when do you leave for the Middle East?" she asked in return.

"Same of you. Won't know until he decides to notify me. I already have my passport, visas, and travel luggage ready to go, but it is a hurry up and wait game I guess."

CHAPTER 28

Two months later, Frank and Nancy were to meet the team in Tucson, Arizona at the Westin La Paloma Resort and Spa. This five star hotel offered its guests the best of everything; golf, swimming pools, massage, great food, workout rooms, sauna, you name it.

Frank and Nancy flew in a day before the rest of the team so that Frank could not only make sure that his team members room reservations were set and there were no glitches, but more importantly, check to see if the mock up chapel had been constructed in the desert area miles south of the hotel. Satisfied that upon their arrival, there would be no snags regarding their rooms, Nancy and Frank decided to hangout by the pool, and finding a table with umbrella, they ordered an early lunch.

Nancy, always watching her figure, ordered a Caesar salad and an ice tea. Frank decided on a BLT with fries and a Bloody Mary. Satisfied with their lunch, they decided to give up their table and moved to two freed up chaise lounges. Putting on their sunglasses, Frank was first to remove his Hawaiian shirt, leaving him wearing his black walking shorts. Nancy removed her sleeveless blouse, revealing the top to one of her bikinis. She had black shorts on also.

She reached into her tote bag, and pulled out a tube of sun-tan lotion and without waiting to be asked, Frank quickly volunteered to apply it to her back. Instead of just rolling over for Frank however, Nancy stood and removed her black shorts showing Frank she had on the matching part of her bikini. After doing so, she then laid on her stomach and Frank went to work. He wondered how many of those other males, obviously acting as peeping toms, ate their hearts outs, seeing what he got to do with Nancy. God, she had an awesome body. Yes, I am probably an egomaniac, but you guys can kiss my ass, he thought.

Nancy reached around and untied her top so that she would not have tan marks.

After about an hour, in which both Frank and Nancy got in a cat nap, they decided that with approaching clouds, it might be cool enough to venture into the desert and check out the "chapel" of the Ark of the Covenant. A mock rendition of the actual site they would be raiding.

They ordered a rent-a-car, a new white Shelby Mustang with blue racing stripes, which Nancy picked out, and headed out to the desert. Nancy drove. Frank, using his GPS, gave directions. Nancy, who usually wants to play music while she was in a car, instead wanted to hear the powerful engine respond to her pressing on the accelerator.

Frank's cellphone rang and he answered. "This is Frank," he said.

Nancy backed off the accelerator pedal in case the sound of the powerful Mustang engine and road noise, might be interfering with Frank's ability to hear.

She heard Frank state, "Yes, yes, I understand. Thank you for the update." There was a lot of silence during the phone call that last maybe 4 minutes in Nancy's estimation.

Frank put the phone in the left front pocket of his Hawaiian shirt and looked at Nancy, saying, "That was one of our contacts in Saudi Arabia. The yacht can arrive within two days of my go ahead. Once that date is given, a timetable will be set up regarding the arrival of the crew members, equipment and ladies. The same thing goes with the truck containing the ATVs." This was the most information Frank had ever shared with Nancy, a sign she felt meant that Frank was not suspicious of her.

"Do you have any idea as to when you will send James and the rest of the team into operation?" Nancy asked. Frank did not respond.

Frank told Nancy to slow down since they would be making a left turn soon. Nancy noticed that any right or left turn from the road they were on, would turn into a road made of sand, cacti, snakes and lizards.

"Turn here," Frank said. "We will continue south for about 5 miles. I will let you know when we are getting close"

Frank could not shake the feeling that they were being followed, yet periodic checks of the rear and side mirrors showed no signs of a tail. Frank was unaware that a tracking device had been placed on the undercarriage of their vehicle eliminating the need for a class surveillance team that Frank might easily spot.

Several miles away, a drone was flying high in the sky monitoring the route being traveled by Frank and Nancy. Once they finished whatever they were up too, FBI agents would visit the area for any evidence they might find and add to their growing intel database.

In a few minutes, Frank did not have to tell Nancy to stop. Both could see a building resembling the chapel of the Ark, surrounded by wrought iron fencing. Both Frank and Nancy were amazed at how closely it mimicked the original building Axum, even down to the windows, which however, were not stained glass.

"Whoever build this mock up did a great job," Frank said.

Nancy just nodded in agreement transfixed at the building she saw.

In the back of a well air conditioned van, agents circled the area on a map where the vehicle stopped. They called in the drone, not wanting to get too close and be spotted.

CHAPTER 29

When they arrived back at the hotel, Nancy saw Jessie, Joe and Ed near the pool bar. They saw Nancy, and Ed waved. Frank noticed Nancy waving and then also saw the three. No Ruben though, Frank thought. James, was already in the air heading to Saudi Arabia and had called Frank to let him know he was at the airport.

Frank motioned that he and Nancy needed five minutes to drop off their stuff into their room and would meet them back at the pool. When they returned, they found that Ruben had joined them .

"Where were you earlier?" Frank asked.

"Oh, I had to scout out the local talent and let them know I was in town for a little while," he replied. "What a stud you are," said Frank, as Nancy, unseen by anyone else, pinched Frank on his ass, thinking to herself that Frank and the team's $500 "therapy session" was still working.

"How are your rooms?" Frank asked. Everyone said great or something meaning the same. Frank continued, “Nancy and I are going to get out of these sweaty clothes and get ready for dinner. How about we meet here at seven and decide on where we want to eat. Everyone agreed, so Nancy and Frank headed up to their room.

A trail of clothes from near the front door to the shower, would have shown anyone who entered their room, that Frank and Nancy were eager to help each other “clean up.” What started as a long passionate hug and kiss, turned into a passionate loving making session standing in the oversized shower. Their love making session culminated with both reaching orgasm with Frank pinning Nancy against a shower wall, and Nancy having her legs wrapped around Frank’s waist. Both spent, Nancy released her legs from Frank’s hips, and the two-stood chest to chest kissing, with Nancy’s arms around Frank’s neck, while his was caressing her tight rear end.

“Frank,” Nancy said. “You know you are the only one, don’t you?”

Frank did not respond but let his long passionate kiss and tongue tell her how he felt about her. Nancy’s thoughts however where hundreds of miles away with James. She was still sad that they had not been able to spend the night together before he departed, but as usual, Frank did not give the order to James to head to the Middle East with any time to spare for a quick rendezvous.

Seven PM came and the team met at the main bar. Frank ordered drinks while Nancy, perused a brochure she got from the front desk, describing the various restaurants in the area. After a little debate, the group of seven decided on the Five Palms Steak and Seafood restaurant a few miles from the hotel. This seemed like the only way to satisfy those that wanted steak or prime rib, while others wanted lobster and crab. No one was disappointed when their main course arrived. Everyone but Ed ordered dessert. When dinner ended, Joe, Jessie, Ruben and Frank ordered an after-dinner drink, while Nancy, Ed and James had coffee or tea.

Frank, feeling that the table they were seating at was secure enough from prying ears, had everyone lean a little closer towards him.

Nancy took the opportunity to put her hand under the table on Frank's knee. Whenever she got the chance, she would stroke his leg and she would see if he would respond. Yes, she knew it was working. God help her if Frank did something similar, for her thoughts were far off on James.

Chapter 30

"Tomorrow morning at 6 AM, we will meet in the lobby and head to the hotel cafe for breakfast. I want us to be on the road enroute to the mock up site, no later than 7- 7:30, so that we can be done with the walk through before the intense heat comes.

Dress like we are just going out to explore the desert." Frank said to the group.

"Shit," said Joe, "back to the damn desert again. Didn't we get enough of the fucking desert in the war?" Frank knew that Joe was not expecting a response, so he went on. "I will have two rent-a-cars waiting for us after breakfast, like the vehicles we used to get here. Ed, seeing Frank and Nancy return earlier in the white Shelby Mustang said, "Hey, can we get a Shelby like you two did earlier?"

"Sure Ed," said Frank. "I want to see you, Ruben and Jessie all squeeze into a Mustang.

"No way, "said Jessie and Ruben.

"I guess that settles the issue," Frank added.

Upon arriving at the chapel, Jessie, and Ruben were both surprised as to how it closely resembled the pictures they had seen.

"Again, we are just going to familiarize ourselves with the exterior of the structure. Your approach, and then you guys can start deciding on who has responsibility for what."

"Is this a timed mock raid Frank?" asked Jessie.

"No," Frank said. "That will come later after some of the equipment you will be using arrives at the hotel.

"It may seem like this is a little overkill, but there is a lot riding on this and unlike most of our black ops, we do not have anything available to come and bail our asses out.

If you get there that evening, and forgot the slightest piece of equipment, or left something up for chance, we are fucked. Everything is riding on this one shot. It's make or break; no second chances."

"And another thing before I forget," Frank seemed as if he was getting upset, so Nancy, quickly stroked him closer to home, at which point, he seemed to calm down.

"I hope that we do not have to take anyone out, but if it is necessary, do so, as quietly as you can. Use your knife if you can, or your hands, but try not to use your Sig, even though it has a silencer. We cannot bring attention to the chapel, even if we luck out and get thunder and lightning that night. Understood?"

Everyone nodded.

After another walk-thru by the group around the perimeter, Frank said, "Ok, let's head ack to the hotel and I will buy everyone a nightcap. They climbed back into their rent-a-cars and began driving back to the hotel. Nancy sat in the back of one cars, a blue Dodge Charger, driven by Ruben, while Joe rode shotgun.

Following them in a fancy red Dodge Challenger, was Ed and Jessie. Frank hoped that this would satisfy Ed's desire to drive a Shelby Mustang that he had seen Nancy drive earlier. At the restaurant Joe said,"Hey Sarge, you seemed a little tense after dinner. Do you think we are going to screw this up?"

"No, Joe," Frank said as Nancy, using the cover of darkness, began touching Frank in the right place getting an instant rise. "This job however, requires timing, being at the right place at the right time, a lot of moving parts, not to forget that we will be operating in several foreign countries. I have total faith in you guys, I just hope that I don't forget something. That is all." With that said, Frank stopped talking, and placed his right hand between Nancy's legs. Fortunately, she was wearing a loose- fitting summer dress. He too, using the cover and darkness and the sound of the engine, moved his hand strategically up Nancy's legs.

Nancy, grabbed Frank's hand and guided it to the right spot, while she snuggled up closer to him and breathed on his neck, quietly panting. Both could hardly wait for the drive back to the hotel to end so that could continue exploring each other in their room.

CHAPTER 31

After breakfast, attended by everyone except Nancy, they climbed into the Jeeps Frank had ordered and headed out to the desert and the site of the mock chapel. Frank decided that Nancy did not need to be there while the group discussed logistics of the actual raid. She instead, would have breakfast on her own and continue to work on adding superfluous bullshit onto everyone's Facebook account and share information with the computer geeks in Saudi Arabia working on websites for the team.

It was much easier to find the site this time around, although Frank did have to use his GPS to determine exactly where to turn off the paved road into the desert. When they arrived, everyone was amazed at the detail that went into the mock chapel. Even the fencing had the L brackets Frank showed them in the slides. The front doors to the chapel, Frank told them, was an educated guess since it is always covered with cloth. Today it was no exception since whoever reconstructed this building had even put cloth over the doors like in the pictures Nancy showed, and like what Frank remembered from his trips to Axum.

The windows were not stained glass, but they seemed to be the exact height and width shown in Nancy's slides, even down to the glass squares, making up each panel. Jessie said that it looked like a Hollywood production set, since, when he looked inside, he could see that it was totally empty: just a shell of a chapel.

Ruben looked inside and said, "Shit, no Ark in here." Everyone laughed.

"Ok, Banshees, here is what I want to cover today," Frank said as he had his team walk to the rear of the chapel. Assume over here are the trees and brushes you will use to conceal your ATVs.

You will approach this area of the fencing. Using the grinder, you will remove a section. After you guys enter the courtyard, replace it, fastening it to a pole with good old duct tape.

Nancy will be in the hotel, located across from the chapel, so she will not be able to view you from her location. For me, I will be walking around to various vantage points, but assume that I will be in the dark regarding your progress, so keep updating Nancy and me.

Once you reach this area, two of you can start working on the glass while the others provide cover. Someone needs to use the Range-R to determine exactly, how many people are inside. Don't forget the gas and hose. You guys will have to decide who's responsible for that. You will score the glass and insert the hose. Use the rag to form a seal around the hose and the glass. Open the gas and keep track of the time.

Once that is complete, you will then make your way around the side of the chapel to the front," Frank was saying this as he walked the team around the side of the chapel to the front door entrance.

Now, here is where it gets a little tricky. You must choose the least amount of C-4 to use to blow one side of the double entrance doors. Nancy and I never got close enough to take any pictures that would allow us to determine the thickness of the door, nor what type of wood they used to make them. We also could not get any pictures of the hinges either. I sure hope that it is a stormy night so no one will take notice of the sound of the detonation.

Now the easy part. The guardian should be out cold. Make sure someone checks on the old man. You do not have to give him a double tap," Frank said as he made a gun out of his right hand, placed it against his forehead, and pulled the make- believe trigger. Everyone laughed. "Remember, we are not in Iraq."

Spread out inside, and using your infrared, find the Ark of the Covenant. If it has poles, take them. If not, use the telescopic one you have in your pack. If you feel you have time, take anything else of value that you can easily take back to the ATVs.

Once you have the package, let Nancy and me know, so that we can start checking out the perimeter for your retreat. Now you will retrace your path, with the last person putting the door you blew off the hinges back in place the best you can. I understand that we don't know the damage the C-4 will do, but it is imperative, that we leave the chapel as normal as possible since, at any time, after the rain stops, the guards will start making their rounds. We don't want them determining that something is amiss too soon, and have them on our trail.

You make it back to the ATVs, secure the package, and drive back to base camp. You will break camp, and driving the ATVs, get back to the truck. Transfer the package to the truck, leave the ATVs, and drive back to the beach and the waiting speed boat.

Since you will be keeping Nancy and me up to date on your progress, I will alert James to pull closer to the shore and pick you and the Ark up.

Questions?" Frank asked, hoping that with all the work he put in the plan, that there would be none. He was not disappointed.

"Ok," let's get back to the hotel so we can relax before lunch and I can check to see if our equipment has arrived. If it has, we will do a mock walk through tomorrow."

CHAPTER 32

Fattah was summoned to the same tent where he once again met with al-Otaibi, Gulmurod Khalimov and Abu Yusaf.

"So, my brother, was your trip a success?" asked al- Otaibi offering Fattah some tea.

"I think so, yes - from the training I have received, I feel it should be an easy job to retrieve the Ark if it is there," Fattah replied.

"Excellent. So please outline for us what you found," said al-Otaibi.

Fattah had many photos and tourist documents that he passed to al-Otaibi who, after studying the material, passed it on to Khalimov and Yusaf. Fattah explained the pictures he had taken in more detail than the tourists documents, feeling that this what the three top leaders wanted to comprehend.

"This is the chapel that supposedly has the Ark. I wrote on the back of several photos, the estimated length and width of the building. As you can see, the only barrier is that fencing that runs along the entire perimeter. I did not see any alarm system nor experienced guards that would hinder a raid. Unfortunately, I did not see the guardian during my visit." With that, Fattah patiently waited while the three individuals continued to study the photos and have short conversations between each other.

There was a brief pause as al-Otaibi seemed to decide what he wanted to say next. "You have done well my brother. We are very impressed with the information you have brought back from your trip. We have decided that you should draw up a plan on how you would attack the chapel. You Fattah, are to pick your team. You decide how many brothers will be needed to successful attack the chapel. Pray to Allah who will give you insight and help you design a plan. Meet with us again here tomorrow afternoon with your strategy. Go now and relax my brother."

Fattah thanked them for placing this responsibility on him, realizing that his "brothers" in the CIA had been correct in their assessment of him being placed in such a role. Upon leaving the tent, and feeling exhausted from his trip, he spend most of his thoughts on how the CIA would stop the raid on the chapel after learning later, his plans for the assault. Perhaps he thought, after a long nap, he could formulate a plan that would result in no civilian causalities, and perhaps his inclusion of being arrested and thus end his undercover operations.

CHAPTER 33

Shit, it was hot, James thought, as he exited the airport after claiming his luggage. Outside he saw two Middle Eastern types, standing together, with one of them holding a sign with his last name. He walked up to them and they both shook his hand while one motioned to a waiting a black stretch limo near the curb.

All right, James thought. First class all the way.

Each of the two men, took a suitcase apiece and placed them inside the trunk of the vehicle. The smaller of the two quickly opened the rear passenger left side door, and James climbed in.

James was not trained to spot a surveillance team, for if he was, he would have seen a man and a woman staring in his direction with one of them holding a camera with a telescopic lens.

Once inside the vehicle, James found several bowls of fruit, some flat bread, and some type of meat and fish to make a sandwich. The window between the front seat and rear was down and the non-driver told James that he would find some beverages in the mini refrigerator. He asked if everything was up to James standards. James assured them that everything was great.

Being hungry from the long flight to Saudi Arabia and the airlines food choices, James helped himself to the spread laid out before him. Opening the refrigerator, he was surprised to find beer as well as hard liquor. Now with a full stomach and a little buzzed from the booze, James decided to put on some headphones and listen to some music and they started their drive to the marina where the yacht was waiting his arrival.

James must have just dozed off because he woke up after the driver of the limo shook his shoulder a few times, calling him James. He woke up and wiped the sleep from his eyes. Placing his sunglasses back on, he exited the limo. Instantly he could smell the sea and hear the sea birds. He also heard music coming from somewhere close by.

There she was, backed into the dock. Damn she was a beauty, thought James, as he got his first glimpse of the yacht he would be sailing. The Saudis and whoever else is bankrolling this operation sure knows what a luxury yacht should look like. He was told by the limo driver, that it was a Le Pharaon 194' custom build yacht, refitted in 2015. It had twin diesel engines and could cruise at 15 knots. There were 4 staterooms as well as rooms for the crew. In total, it could easily sleep twelve and as many as sixteen.

This was the type of super yacht James had dreamed of sailing while attending maritime school. He walked around the yacht and saw that it also had assorted water toys, jet skis, a jet boat, and even a banana that could easily tow 4 adults. The master cabin was huge and the gourmet kitchen was outstanding. It had an oversized hot tub, a huge bar, a room with an 84" flat screen television. The command bridge was stat of the art. He just hoped he would remember what everything did. Bottom line, except for not having a helicopter pad, it had everything a "filthy rich American playboy" should have.

When he had finished his self-guided tour of the yacht and returned to the main deck, he saw two females and three males, take off their shoes, and climb aboard the yacht. The limo driver, speaking in Arabic, pointed to James, and they walked up to greet him.

Before they could extend their hands for a shake, James said that he did not speak, nor understand Arabic. The taller of the two newly boarded males said in perfect English, "We all speak English quite well captain."

James estimated their ages to be around 25-30 years old.

He had to admit, it felt great being referred to as "captain."

Everyone shook hands. The taller male explained the jobs each crew member was assigned. The two females took care of maintenance of the rooms, laundry, drinks and meal servings. One male was trained as a gourmet chef and obviously would oversee the kitchen. The other two would be go-to crew hands for whatever needed to be done, such as the docking duties, and the launching and retrieving of water toys. The one who did the initial introduction, said that his name was Bashir, and that he has yacht training, and that he would be assisting James with piloting the yacht when James was sleeping or otherwise engaged. Almost on cue, the driver and passenger of the limo said goodbye to James and departed from the yacht. followed by the arrival of a second limo. This one was about the same size as the one he rode in, but white in color. The driver of the limo got out and opened the door on the same side that the yacht was moored.

A pair of gorgeous legs appeared as the door fully opened. If the female attached to these legs, looked half as good, this was going to be a dream cruise, James thought. He was not disappointed. She had long blonde hair and an outstanding body. She obviously worked out. Wearing a tight pair of form fitting white pants and a sleeveless blue blouse, her tanned body fit in to the marina environment. She stood near the rear of the limo allowing the second female passenger to exit.

The second female was also equally as gorgeous. She was a brunette, hair in a ponytail, slightly shorter than the first, wearing the shortest pair of shorts James had ever seen. She had high heel shoes on so actually, she would be a lot shorter than the first female. Wearing a yellow tank top and sporting a green visor cap, she could easily pass for a fashion model.

Finally, the third female slid out of the limo. Initially James thought that it was Nancy since she had long jet black hair, also in a ponytail, with a red bow keeping it in place. She, like the others, had a pair of sunglasses but wore no cap or hat. Wearing white short-shorts, sandals, and a checkered colored blouse, she, like the others, was stunning. She had a killer body and was the tallest of the three. The three did not initially start for the yacht, but instead, waited for the limo driver who was solo, to retrieve their luggage. One of the male crew members seeing this, immediately put on his shoes, left the yacht, and helped the driver with their luggage.

Satisfied that their luggage was accounted for, the three females started for the yacht. The crew member with some of the luggage, asked the girls to please remove their shoes before boarding, which they did. One of the other female crewmembers, greeted the ladies, and offered any assistance in boarding the yacht.

James was observing all of this from the command bridge, and decided to wait until the ladies had been escorted aboard to their staterooms and refreshed themselves, before he would introduce himself. There would be plenty of time for formal introductions during cocktail hour and dinner. He did have visions however, of making love with each one of them235.

CHAPTER 34

James had been relieved by Bashir, so he went to his cabin, took a cool shower and a short nap.

He instructed one of the female crewmembers to wake him at 5 P.M. and asked her to invite the three ladies who were onboard to meet him in the lounge for drinks before dinner.

Hearing the knock on his stateroom's door, James thanked whoever woke him up and took another cold shower. Fresh and now shaven, he dressed in his Hawaiian dress shirt, and white pants, leaving the top several buttons open of his shirt. He combed his blonde hair, made sure his deodorant was working, slapped on some of his favorite aftershave lotion, and gave himself one last look in the mirror. He was wondering the whole time, which of the ladies he would entertain in his room that night.

There was a little feeling of guilt between his lustful thoughts and his love for Nancy, but, who knows what she could be doing with Frank right now?

When he entered the lounge, the three ladies where already present and if on command, all stood to great him. The first to come forward was the blonde who was wearing a very expensive silk blouse, that revealed a black lace bra, and a wrap-around skirt. While extending her hand she said, "Hello captain, my name is Danica. I am very happy to be with you on this cruise. You have such a lovely boat." She had a thick accent and James thought she was probably Russian, so he asked her such.

She said while blushing,"No, I am Czechoslovakian.""Nice to meet you," James said The female with the raven black hair came forward, but instead of extending her hand, hugged James tight to her chest, and whispered her name into his right ear, biting down lightly on his earlobe, "I'm Monique." She too had an accent, and he knew instantly that she was French. "Nice to meet you, Monique," James said, as he felt his manhood starting to stir. She was wearing a sleeveless white blouse, so shear that James could see her firm breasts and erect nipples. Her pants were so tight, James wondered how she got into them. The final lady waited for Monique to walk a short distance from James before she approached. Her green eyes were mesmerizing. James guessed that while the other two females introduced themselves, the brunette watched, evaluated their "technique" of introduction and decided on how she could make a bigger impression. She had changed from her yellow tank top to a sheer blue sleeveless top. She was not wearing a bra either and James did not need to imagine what her breasts looked like. She slowly wrapped her left arms around James and then, grabbed his left hand and placed it on her right breast. Then, slowly, she kissed him so soft with a lot of tongue action. When she finished, she said, "I'm Agnetha, and before you ask, the accent you hear is from Sweden."

Damn again, James thought, the Saudis and whoever else is bankrolling this heist, went first class all the way. First class flight, first class limo, first class yacht, and now, wow, first class ladies.

One of the female crewmembers came forward asking for drink orders. While this was happening, the other female crewmember brought in some hors d'oeuvres. The ladies surrounded James, bringing the hors d'oeuvres to him. He felt like he was living some of the movie scenes in which the prince is surrounded by his harem, satisfying all his needs.

When the drinks they ordered arrived, the ladies decided to take their seats, finally giving James a chance to catch his breath. To say that he was turned on, would be an understatement. The "co-captain" appeared in the lounge and asked to speak with James. The captain asked the ladies to excuse him, while he walked a short distance away from the group to talk privately.

"Captain, I wanted to report that we will be able to set sail at daybreak if that is what you desire." He waited for James' response, expecting a thank you or some type of acknowledgement for a job well done.

Instead, he got an unexpected answer in which James explained that the next morning, they would have three additional passengers, his friends from the United States, and would not set sail for a few days after that. Seeing a sign of disappointment in the "co-captain's" face, James told him that he had done a great job preparing for the trip ahead, but for now, he should just relax and enjoy what the yacht and marina had to offer. This seemed to satisfy the "co-captain" who seemed to appreciate the acknowledgement of his captainship abilities.

To make sure that he repaired any deflation of the "co-captain's" ego, James said, "Ladies, I would like to introduce to you my second-in-command." James could not remember the co-captain's name, and even if he could, he probably would mispronounce it, so instead he added, "he pretty much runs the ship." All the ladies said something flattering and James knew he was on target since the co-captain bowed his head and sheepishly looked at James and said, "Thank you, Captain, with your permission, I will return to the command bridge." James nodded in agreement.

The crewmember who earlier brought the hors d'oeuvres, announced to James and his guests, that dinner was served. Everyone waited for James to rise, and then they all retreated to the outdoor dining area. There was a slight breeze that made it prefect for outdoor dining. The female crewmembers did an outstanding job decorating the table. With the gorgeous ladies to the right and left of James, anyone who maybe surveilling them, would conclude that James was a playboy, and one lucky bastard at the same time.

The girls made small talk during dinner which, was excellent. The final course, desert of Baba au Rum was offered, was as good as any five-star restaurant James had ever dined in. Some of the ladies talked about how impressed they were with the yacht. Others wanted to know about James, the United States, or how great the food tasted. Wine continued to flow during all the courses served, including dessert.

Once everyone was satisfied, James suggested that they get another round of drinks and then they would go to the various hot spots in the Marina, as Frank had instructed. James threw money around like it was no tomorrow and made sure that he and the girls were the center of attention. The owners of those places he visited with his "harem" were excited at seeing this American playboy spend money in their establishments, but the local Saudi females that were out and about, looked at James and his ladies with disgust. Frank was right. Finally satisfied that he did as Frank wanted, James told the girls that it was time to head back to the yacht.

Once they arrived, James suggested that they hit the hot tube located aft of the yacht. All the ladies agreed and excused themselves to get their swimwear. James also retreated to his stateroom and changed into his trunks. He was the first one to arrive at the hot tub and was greeted by a crewmember who gave him his vodka martini. He had just taken a sip of his drink when he heard the three ladies talking as they approached. He turned and saw them all wearing the skimpiest bikinis he had ever seen, but he was not complaining.

Each of the ladies were given a drink, like the one they had first ordered that evening. They climbed into the hot tube, all describing how nice and warm the water was. The round tub easily handled the four of them.

More small talk took place until Agnetha stood out of the water and removed her bra. Not to be outdone, Monique and Danica followed. Agnetha, who was directly across from James, walked over to him and climbed on his lap, straddling him.

Danica followed and was now seated to James right, while Monique now sat to his left. Before James realized it, there was not one part of his body that was not being explored by his "harem." James noticed the bottoms of all three bikinis floating on the surface of the hot tub. He knew he would sleep great tonight. He knew the French word for a threesome was ***ménage à trois***, but if he was right, he would be with three women, not just two. What the hell he thought, as he asked Monique, what the French word was, that he was looking for. She got close again to his ear and said as she licked him, saying so sexy, "partie carrée"

CHAPTER 35

The next morning James woke up and found Danica, Monique and Agnetha lying in his bed with him being in the center. What a night he thought, from what he could remember. He glanced at this Rolex and saw that it was 10 A.M. His stirring to look at his watch had required him to move his right arm from under the head of Danica. She started to wake up, glanced at James, stretched up to give him a passionate kiss, and then she fell back asleep.

He could slide out of the bed with only minor movements detected by Monique or Agnetha, and after finding his clothes from the night before, dressed and made his way to the command bridge. He checked in with the "co-captain" and learned that everything was fine and that the expected guests had not arrived yet. James told him that if they did not arrive today, for sure, they would be here by tomorrow. He told the "co-captain" that once he and the ladies had breakfast and relaxed for a while, he wanted to take the yacht out of the marina so that the girls and he could enjoy some of the water toys. The "co-captain" got a huge smile since now he could show off his navigational skills to James. With that said, James headed to the galley to get some coffee and something to eat from the chef, before the ladies joined him for breakfast.

The chef put on a fantastic gourmet breakfast. You could choose from a variety of entrees. James opted for scrambled eggs, bacon, sausage, potatoes, whole wheat toast, and freshly squeezed orange juice.

The girls began arriving, all greeting James with long passionate kisses. Each had decided to wear their bikinis and cover-ups. He learned later that one of the female crewmembers had told them what was on the agenda today.

While each of them continued with their breakfast, James went up to the command bridge and met with Bashir. Now he could remember the guy's name. Oh well, he thought, I had my mind on other things yesterday evening when I drew a blank in remembering his name.

"Ok, Bashir, let's see what this lady can do." Taking that as a command to take the yacht out, Bashir called to the other crewmembers who quickly followed his commands to undock the boat, pull in the lines, and maneuver the yacht from her berth. Banshee did one hell of a job, James thought. He wasn't sure if he would remember how to do it when it fell on him.

Bashir, only occasionally looking at a chart, sailed to a part of the coast that had sheer cliffs that acted as a windbreak when anchored to the south. He instructed that the bow anchor be dropped, but not until his male crewmembers, had taken the rubber raft boat to the cliff and attached cables back to the yacht. This created a triangle type anchor system for the back of the boat which the bow anchor kept it in position.

The day was spent with James and the girls riding jet skis, driving the jet boat while towing the girls on the banana, tubing and finding an island that had a sandy beach to stretch out and relax until lunch time. When they returned to the yacht, Bashir informed him that his guests had arrived and are waiting at the marina. With that, James told the girls to get dressed to meet his friends and that lunch would be a little late until they got onboard and settled in.

The crewmembers, again using the rubber boat, removed the cables from the rocks on the cliff and returned to the yacht. That done, one of them raised the bow anchor and Bashir maneuvered the yacht masterfully. The other male deck hands secured the yacht to its mooring without any line hitting the water. On the dock were Jessie, Ed, Joe and Ruben. They were all dressed like wealthy Americans out for a good time. Each had on their own variation of what a wealthy American would wear for an ocean outing. Since part of the plan was to later purchase sport fishing equipment, each only had their own luggage to bring onboard.

Ed was the first one on board followed by Jessie, Ruben and finally Joe. The ladies came to greet them, laughing and holding on to each of them. Ed, for once, was tongue-tied. Jessie instantly took a liking to Danica and by their body language, Ed already made a claim for Agnetha and Joe targeted Monique. No one initially approached Ruben.

James realized that mathematically, he and Ruben were the odd ones out. Oh well, he thought, after I get them to their next destination and drop them off, he will again have all three ladies. His harem would be back together again, worshipping him and all his desires.

Ruben was not going to be without a woman he said, so he started searching the yacht for the female crewmembers, and sure enough, he scored, not with one, but with both.

For the sake of anyone possibly spying on them, they stuck to the script Frank gave them; partying loudly into the night on the yacht, making several scenes while onshore, throwing around lots of money, and then returning to the yacht.

The next day on cue, the four guys without the ladies, went into the marina and bought the most expensive fishing equipment they could buy. They got into conversations with all the fishing gear store employees about what they hoped to catch, the strategies and bait they should use, and the best areas where they should fish in. But, the four of them knew that none of the fishing gear would ever be24u6 sed.

On the way back to the yacht, Frank called James on the burner phone. It was predicted that by next week a huge storm was expected to hit the area of Axum bringing a lot of rain. The order to execute the plan was made. James told Bashir that they would start their cruise towards the Red Sea at daybreak. Bashir acknowledged and told the other crewmembers, minus the females, who had already hooked up with Ruben in his cabin.

CHAPTER 36

At daybreak, both James and Bashir, both in the command bridge, headed out of the marina towards Eritrea. It was just another fun run to check out the yacht and keep up appearances for the locals. The yacht maneuvered flawlessly. When both engines were at max speed, you could not ask for a smoother ride, but James instructed Bashir to adjust the speed, so that they would arrive at their destination in the early afternoon, not earlier or later. Joe was the first one up, followed by Ed and Jessie.

James asked them how they slept and they each looked at each other with smiles. Ruben was the last to arrive. "Sorry Ruben, but the women chose us," bragged Ed. "Not a problem gringo. My ladies took care of me just fine," as the two female crewmembers came into the lounge area with coffee. They each looked at Ruben and blushed. The ladies had on tight white shorts and both had decided to let their hair down. "Son of a bitch, Ruben scored a threesome," said Jessie.

"It will go down in my book, as one of the best nights of my life," said Ed. Joe and Jessie just nodded. When the ladies arrived, James told them that unless it was too windy, they should have breakfast at the aft of the yacht again. Everyone thought that this was a great idea, so each lady, grabbed the arms of their bedtime partner and headed off. James said he would join them shortly.

Frank called James again while he was on his way from the command bridge to meet the others and get some coffee and breakfast. Frank wanted all four of them to meet in James stateroom for a private phone conversation at 11:30. James understood and told Frank they would be there.

Everyone was enjoying their breakfast while the guys, minus James and Ruben, continued to flirt with their "dates." After grabbing something to eat and finishing his third cup of coffee, James told Jessie, Ed, Joe, and Ruben, Frank's request. They all said they would be there.

On schedule, James phone rang with everyone in his stateroom. James answered the phone and said that everyone was present. He then said he was going to put the phone on speaker. "Hello Frank, yes we are all here" James said again, "Can you hear us?"

Frank responded, "yes."

"Anyone had problems up to this point?" Frank asked. Everyone said no. "Good," Frank said. "Nancy and I have checked in and we have noticed no changes from what we saw the last time we were here. Somedays there are four volunteer guards, other days maybe five. It has started to rain off and on and as predicted, they do not like to make their rounds when the rain is coming down.

"We took more pictures today and the approach at the rear of the chapel is still the best avenue for you to use. There is enough foliage and growth to provide you with cover for yourselves and the ATVs. I talked with our contacts that will meet you at a marina in Djibouti. This will be your last stop until James gets you to the coast of Eritrea. They will meet you there late tonight to transfer your equipment and the gas. Someone should entertain your lady friends while the transfer of equipment takes place. The less they know the better. Your crewmates are ok and they can assist. Ok, so far, so good. Until I call James telling you to execute, just relax and continue the charades as you did in Saudi Arabia." With that, Frank hung up.

Late that afternoon, they reached Djibouti.

The marina was smaller than the one they left, but there were still several large yachts moored, so the arrival of their 194 foot Le Pharaon did not cause a commotion. James guessed that there were a lot of rich Middle Easterners who tried to outdo each other by purchasing larger and larger custom yachts. What a life.

Night came and after some partying to keep up the appearance of their wealthy lifestyle onboard, the ladies retired to their "boyfriends" cabins while the five waited up in the top deck to watch for the approach of their equipment.

At approximately 1:30, a black Mercedes van drove up near the yacht's berth. Two men got out and spotted Jessie, Ed, Joe, Ruben and James and deckhands coming towards them. They got out of the Mercedes and opened the rear doors.

It did not take long, with so much help, to transfer the gear onboard. In fact, the two people from the Mercedes did not have to do anything but wait for the equipment to be unloaded, so that they could shut the doors and depart. Now, the Banshees waited for Frank's call.

Chapter 37

The next day, James ordered that the yacht again head out of the marina for more fun with the girls and the water toys. Of course, Ed, Joe, Ruben and Jessie were game. They could hardly wait to see the girls that they had not hooked up with barely clothed. They were not disappointed.

Lunch was served after James maneuvered the yacht close to a small island used to break the slight wind the was picking up. Ed, Joe, and their "dates," except Ruben, decided to jump over the side into the warm water. Jessie and his "date" returned to their room for whatever.

Ruben, learning from his girls that this was the time they took their naps before the rest of their afternoon-evening duties, decided to join them. None of them really got any sleep.

Before cocktail hour, Frank called James and again asked everyone to meet in Jame's room. On speaker phone again, Frank said that there was a slight change in plans but nothing major. Transporting the four ATVs, would require a larger truck and that might be suspicious entering the marina area, so here is he wanted them to do.

Frank then said, "The weather is getting nasty here and the forecast is for more of the same. This evening, James, I will send you the coordinates you need to follow. As you guys have done for several days now, you will set out once again for what the locals believe is another day of fun in the sun. You will be heading from the Gulf of Aden into the Red Sea and almost immediately, the coastal waters of Eritaea. Find a place to anchor the yacht. Ed, Joe, Ruben, Jessie, you guys will place your equipment and the gas in the jet boat and head to the shoreline. Tie down the boat, secure the keys and you should easily spot the large 4x4 truck containing the ATVs inside. Keys will be in the sun visor of the truck.

"How will we know where to beach the boat?" Joe asked.

"They told me that there is only one possible approach to the shoreline and the truck will be located up a short hill directly above," replied Frank.

"Once you cross over into Ethiopia, you should continue by truck until you are about one klick out from the chapel. That is where you will set up your base camp. The walkie-talkies you have, will be in distance range so that you can communicate with Nancy and me. You can ditch them once you get closer to the chapel and will replace them with your normal communication gear.

Ok troops, it's show time!" With that said, Frank hung up. Frank never liked to say good luck. His philosophy of "prepare for the worst, so when it happens, you won't be surprised" did not allow for phases such as "good luck."

James turned the yacht over to his Bashir and told the chef that if possible, he would like to have an earlier dinner this evening, say 4 P.M. and have the final course by six. The chef said that that would not be a problem.

A sense of anticipation seemed to be felt among the five of them. Even the ladies could sense the change when the guys returned to the lounge area.

Danica, in her darling Czechoslovakian accent, asked if everything will alright. James and the other four assured her that things were fine and asked the crewmember if they could get some drinks. She took their orders and after leaving for a short time, returned with something to eat to tie them over till dinner.

Dinner was another culinary masterpiece followed by after dinner drinks. Joe, who over the last several days had a bad case of sunburn, said, as he took his "partner," that he was going to call it an early night. The others followed his lead; mostly for sexual desires, but also with realization that it maybe a few days without any real sleep. The sacrifices they must make Jessie thought as he closed the door to his room, watching his date, take off her clothes.

CHAPTER 38

"Hello, this is Agent Loomis. I would like to speak with Mr. Delaney please."

"One moment please and I will connect you," the receptionist said.

"Agent Loomis, how are you?" Delaney said as soon as he answered his phone.

"Good, and you?" Loomis responded.

"Great, thank you for calling me back. There has been a lot of activity recently by one of your subjects in the Middle East and I think it would be beneficial if you and your team met with me again if you are free," Delaney said.

"Yes, we also have some information to share. What is a good time and date for you?" Loomis inquired.

"Does tomorrow morning around nine work for you and your team?" he asked.

"If you promise to have the coffee and sweet rolls ready again, it will be easy to get my colleagues there tomorrow," she said, holding back a laugh.

"That can be arranged. See you tomorrow agent," and without waiting for a reply, Delaney hung up.

The next morning upon entering the conference room, as promised, coffee, herbal tea, sweet rolls and the addition of donuts were awaiting them. Delaney entered and helped himself also. This time the laptop and projector were already set up for his presentation. Loomis thought that after they left the last time, someone got their ass chewed out and learned their lesson.

"Well, who would like to go first? Delaney asked. "Perhaps we should since you probably have a lot more valuable information that we do," responded Loomis.

This time, Flores, seated closest to Delaney, handed him some photos. The first displayed a photo of an almost exact replica of the small little chapel located in Axom.

"Where was this taken?" asked Delaney.

"In the desert south of Tucson, Arizona. Every been there, sir?" asked Flores.

"No, I have not, and seeing this, it will not be on my bucket list," Delaney said with a smile.

Delaney studied the photo and then, turned on his laptop and projector and search for an earlier slide taken by an Interpol agent in Axom. Finding it, he held up the photo shown by Flores and compared the two images. "Damn, it is almost an exact duplicate," he said. "How did you find this?" he asked.

"We had a loose tail on Silva and Dr. Harding and he led us right to it. After they left we moved in and photographed the place. We were fortunate to get in and out before a sandstorm came in which removed any signs of tire tracks," Flores answered.

Flores continued, "The next day, Silva, minus Dr. Harding, returned with the rest of the Banshees. After an initial walk through, they began practicing their raid on the mock up chapel. They returned three days in a row refining their every move." Flores looked at agent Loomis to make sure he should continue. Reading her eyes, he went on. "High altitude surveillance shots did not show us much, other than how we suspect they will advance on the chapel."

"Interesting," Delaney said.

Loomis motioned to McCormick who took over the FBI's presentation. "If you notice in the photos, James Fielding is not in the group. A team followed him to the airport where he boarded a plane to Riyadh. That is where our tail of the suspect ended." McCormick first looked at Loomis and then to Delaney. Loomis took this opportunity to fill in the remaining information they had to date.

"Silva and Harding as well as the Banshees, left Tucson following their practice raids and returned to business as normal. There have been no other signs of activity so we assume that Frank is waiting for something before he gives the order to execute. We believe that this will occur when he and Harding travel back to Ethiopia, if that is part of his plan." With that, Loomis stared at Delaney indicating that this was all the information they had.

"Well, actually, we believe that Frank has started the plan, or at least some of the initial steps," stated Delaney. He turned on the laptop and projector which showed James Fielding arriving at the Riyadh airport. Your phone call alerting us that Fielding was flying out to Riyadh made it extremely easy to set up surveillance at the airport to capture his arrival.

Here he is greeted by Halabi's men who drove him to this luxury yacht. More individuals showed up at the yacht. Delaney stopped to sip some coffee and then he advanced to the next slide. These next individuals we believe are going to be part of the deck crew. There is no way one person could maneuver this size vessel."

The next several slides got the attention of both Flores and McCormick for they showed various close-up shots of three very beautiful women exiting a limo like what had delivered Fielding earlier.

"I can only guess what their professions are, but from this shot of Fielding's face, he must have felt blessed," chucked Delaney, while everyone, including Loomis, laughed.

"Somewhere, Agent Loomis, I recall either hearing or reading, that Silva wants to use the rainy season of Ethiopia as the best time to carry out the raid. Is that correct? asked Delaney.

"Yes sir, we believe that he will start the operation between June and August, when the area receives a tremendous amount of rainfall. For us currently, all we can do is track the movements of Frank, Nancy and the rest of his team. Once we see movement, we will alert you and your agency. Is there anything that the FBI can do for Interpol now? Loomis asked.

"No, it looks like, with the exception of Fielding playing on his yacht, there is nothing any of our agencies can do at the present but watch and wait," responded Delaney.

Just then Agent Loomis's cellphone went off. She excused herself which invited Delaney to motion to the other agents that there was more coffee and sweet rolls. They did not have to be asked twice.

Before they could refill their coffee and sit down with their donuts, Loomis quickly re-entered the conference room. "Wait no more! The Banshees are all headed to the airport, luggage in hand," she stated ecstatically looking at Delaney who instantly got a smile on his face.

Without hesitation, Delaney dialed an unknown number and alerted the person who answered that the subjects were in play and to begin watching the Riyadh airport.

Chapter 39

James thought that it was strange, leaving the gulf and now entering the Red Sea. The water was smooth as glass and the moon was full, yet, according to Frank, they had down-pour after down-poor in Axum. He and Bashir, took turns navigating the yacht, while also taking time as lookout. Except for a few large oil tankers and cargo ships, they had the entire sea to themselves.

At the horizon, the sun was starting to rise. James instructed one of the female crewmembers to wake the chef and have him created a light breakfast just for the males. He also asked her to lightly wake up Ed, Joe, Ruben and Jessie. As it turned out, the three of them opened the door to their respective rooms as the sound of her approach. They were ready.

The female crewmember knew where Ruben was and when she knocked on that door, could hear someone climbing out of bed in a hurry. The door opened and it was Ruben. She gave him a kiss, seeing her co-crewmember gather a sheet over her breasts.

After eating and leaving Bashir in charge of finding the exact coordinates to drop anchor, the five of them went down to the area where the jet boat was stored. Everyone checked and rechecked, as they had done so many times before, making sure that all the necessary equipment had been stored securely in the interior of the boat. With enough light illuminating the approaching shoreline, they could hear the anchor and chain leave the ship for its resting spot on the bottom of the sea.

No one said anything. They each shook hands with James and told him to take care of their women. "Don't worry," said James, "I will take good care of them." Boy, if they only knew, James thought, with a smile on his face that he tried to hide. With that, they lowered the speed boat into the calm water, climbed in, and set off for the shoreline and the heist of all time.

As they got closer to the shore, they saw that there really was only one place where they could safely beach the craft. Most of the shore had rocks jutting out of the water, meaning that there where probably rocks hiding underneath. One decent hit on the fiberglass of their boat, and the mission would be over.

But, there was, just as predicted, one area, wide enough for the boat, appearing to have a sandy area to land. Joe, who was driving the boat could time it just right. The waves broke heavy as they approached and Joe had a hard time controlling her, but at the exact right moment, he gunned the engine and with the help of the surf, slid right in on the beach. Success.

Ed jumped out of the boat first, and using two ropes tied to the bow, secured them to two large boulders. Meanwhile, Jessie, dropped the stern anchor. Satisfied that the boat would be secure for a long time, Jessie and Joe began unloading their gear on the beach. Ruben climbed up the short sandbar to the top and almost in a straight line from the boat, and found the large truck. Whoever parked it there must have realized that there was only one place for them to beach their craft, so it made their job easy.

Ed climbed down the sand dune and told the rest, that the truck was directly up the little hill. The equipment was divided amongst them and up they went. The truck was huge and reminded them of trucks used during World War II, but it beat walking. They pulled back the canvas of the truck and saw the four ATVs. Jessie decided that he would drive the truck and climbed into the driver seat. He pulled down the visor and five sets of keys fell to his lap. One was different than the other four so he assumed it was for the truck. He put one of the other four key sets in his camouflage front pocket and gave the other three sets to Ed, who could later, give a set to Joe and Ruben.

Joe had decided that due to the size of Jessie and Ed, he would ride much more comfortably in the back with Ruben and the ATVs. Ruben had already made that decision and had climbed into the rear of the truck.

Putting the key into the ignition, Jessie fired the truck up. Ed, using a GPS, directed Jessie via back roads into Ethiopia. So far, so good.

The roads were horrendous with pot holes everywhere, so Jessie had no choice but to drive slowly. It would be a major setback if they blew an axle or anything non-repairable in the field, that would strand them out here with no way to get to Axum. After all, the ATVs only had the gas that is in their tanks. There was no way they could travel the distance that remained if that was all they had. No, thought Jessie, slow and steady.

Meanwhile, Ruben and Joe worried about the damn ATVs shifting and crushing them in the back of the truck. So, every time Jessie hit a pot hole, he received several shouts of profanity. Of course, Jessie had heard these words before and just laughed. Ed did the same.

CHAPTER 40

"U*nit 9, this is is unit 10. Two subjects have exited a cab and are entering the airport. They're moving.*"

Agent Loomis was driving a rental car with McCormick, while Flores was in another rental with a female agent. Loomis elected to use rental cars since Frank would easily spot their bureau cars. Running on parallel streets so as not to be notices, it was easy for Loomis and the other tailing vehicle to realize that the cabs destination was the airport. This eliminated any need to follow too close. Besides, once they arrived at the airport would be more than obvious that they were going to make their way to Axum.

Agent Loomis waited until she was notified by a team of FBI agents in the terminal, that the two subjects had arrived and checked in for a flight destined to Ethiopia. This was it they all felt. Once it was confirmed that their flight had taken off and they were onboard, Loomis called the cellphone of Delaney.

He quickly answered announcing his name. Loomis identified herself and stated that the subjects were in play and passed on the investigation to his agency.

His response was, "I will keep you posted," and with that, once again not waiting for a comeback, he hung up.

In Idaho, a swarm of FBI agents hit Frank's cabin. It was so isolated that Agent Loomis, who gave them the go-ahead, wasn't worried about being observed and notifying Silva. Loomis received a phone call from the Idaho FBI SAC that they were in the cabin and that she would contact Loomis once they finished up.

Loomis had no idea what they might find in Silva's cabin. The FBI had also secured a search warrant for Frank seldom used apartment in New York. The decision was made to hold off on executing search warrants on the residences of Dr. Harding, and the rest of the Banshees including Fielding's place.

Agent Loomis released her team and invited them to join her for a night cap. They all indicated that they had prior commitments so she hit a local bar she liked alone. Downing one vodka martini, she began nursing a second one trying to visualize how this long and complicated investigation would end. She was sad that almost all the action will take place in a small town of Axum, Ethiopia, well out of the jurisdiction of her agency.

She also wondered if Frank and the Banshees, as well as Dr. Harding, would actually find the physical

Ark of the Covenant. Born and raised a Catholic and having attended Catholic school through high school, she remembered all the stories in the Bible about the awesome power of the Ark. Of course, when the famous Indiana Jones Raiders of the Lost Ark came out, she could hardly wait to view it, and once she did, it stirred her imagination at the time.

She saw a good-looking man come up to the bar and if she was not mistaken, it seemed like he gave her more than a second glance. She will see if he makes a move. Meanwhile her thoughts returned to their investigation. What if Frank and his group hit the chapel and find nothing. What would they have as far as a case? Sure, doing so probably violated a dozen or more international statues which Delaney and Interpol would follow-up one, but what about the FBI? What would they have to show for their efforts? Well she guessed, they could put the screws to James Fielding regarding his actions at the U.S. Customs yard and see if he would rollover. They had Ed so that was not an issue. He had delivered his part of the bargain so he would probably walk.

As for Frank and his Banshees, she would work them against each other and if nothing comes out of that, she would arrange for Ed to lead the army, ATF and Interpol to the hidden case and try to make a case out of that.

Dr. Nancy Harding, however, would be the hardest to implicate. She could simply state that she was never aware of Frank and his team's criminal activity being so blind by Frank and their love for each other. She had traveled with him to Axom to further her research into the location of the Ark and had no idea what so ever, that behind her back, Frank had planned to steal the Ark. Her reputation might be ruined or at least a little tarnished, but Loomis believed that she would rebound. All she had to do is shake that cute little ass of hers and she would be set.

Chapter 41

It was really coming down in Axum and neither Nancy nor Frank saw any of the armed volunteer guards. To keep up with their appearance and cover story, they decided to walk to the only place nearby were you could get breakfast this early in the morning. Even though it was raining hard, it was a warm rain and very humid.

Nancy wore a white top and dark pants, while Frank wore a white shirt and matching white pants. There were no Christian pilgrims outside in the downpour nor, for that matter, was anyone walking around anywhere without cover. Normally, when the weather was clear, even if the temperature was in the triple digits, hundreds of pilgrims could be seen, dressed in their traditional white gabbi or Netella, a fancier version the Ethiopian women's Kemis, which was a combination of a dress (Kemis) and netella, which had borders of colored embroidered woven crosses..

Initially Frank thought that perhaps Nancy should try to blend in and wear a white gabbi and well as him, maybe passing off as pilgrims, but, due to the many trips they had made there prior, it was easier to keep up the facade of being two American researchers. They arrived at the café and placed their order. The service left a lot to be desired, and the menu did not give a person much choice for breakfast. But, Frank thought, what was the rush. At this moment, Frank and Nancy realized that, if everything was going as planned, Jessie, Joe, Ruben and Ed would be crossing over into Ethiopia about now. Frank verified that with a glance at this watch.

"Relax babe, you came up with a great plan, leaving nothing to chance." Nancy said. She continued, "Your guys are not only highly trained by you, but you have all practiced repeatedly, until they could do it in their sleep.

"Ok, we just crossed over into Ethiopia," said Jessie to Ed. Ed pounded on the rear window and when Joe and Ruben turned, he gave them both the thumbs up sign.

"About another hour and we should be at the location where we can set up our base camp and call Frank," said Jessie.

After breakfast, Frank and Nancy picked up some magazines and newspapers and slowly walked back to their room. There was no sign of the rain letting up, just what Frank wanted. While approaching the hotel, they could not keep their eyes off the chapel. There appeared to be one light or candle on inside, but no movement could be seen. Holding hands, they entered the hotel where Frank purchased a Coca Cola and Nancy a flavored diet tea drink.

Inside their room, Frank looked at this watch again. "They should be getting close to where they will set up their base camp," he said to Nancy. She did not respond, but Frank could see that she heard him. Lying on their bed, Frank turned on the television set knowing that even though the hotel supposedly had satellite, their reception would be bad. He didn't really care, it was more for some "white noise" in the background.

Nancy turned on her laptop and was busy reading something. There they were, the masterminds of the biggest theft the world would soon learn of, and one was glancing at a newspaper he could not read, while the other, only a few feet away, was typing away on her computer, as if she were at home in the states.

Finally, either out of boredom or just wanting Frank to hold her, Nancy closed the computer lid and put her head-on Frank's chest. Her head rose and fell with each of his breaths. Frank threw the newspaper aside and began running his fingers through Nancy's hair like he always did. He swore he heard Nancy "purr" so he slid down a little so his face was across from hers and their eyes met. Kissing started, leading to touching, leading to passion, leading to lovemaking, and then the return to waiting.

CHAPTER 42

Loomis's phone rang on the nightstand of the motel room. It took her a few moments to realize where she was and whom she was with.

He stirred as she got out of bed and answered the phone as she walked into the bathroom. She saw her reflection in the mirror and saw that she was naked.

"Agent Loomis," she answered.

"Agent Loomis, this is Stevenson, SAC up here in Idaho. We just finished the search of Silva' cabin. We found a space under a floorboard that he was using to secure some of his property. We found over $150,000 in currency and some maps. The search warrant instructed us to collect all maps so we did. Other than that, the place was pretty clean. We found a few articles of female clothing in a closet and feminine hygiene products in the master bathroom upstairs, but that's about it."

"Do you still have access to the maps? Loomis asked.

"Sure, wait a minute," he said. She could hear him yell at someone and then heard the rustling of paper. "Yeah, I have all of them here. What do you need?'

"Just start pulling out one map at a time and tell me what you believe it is showing," Loomis requested. "Ok, the first map, oops, some picture fell out – hang on. This map is of, let's see, a town called Axom. There is a large red circle surrounding what looks like some streets or pathways. The pictures show a mission, church or chapel. Does that mean anything to you? he asked.

"Yes," Loomis answered. "That was their target in Ethiopia. Are all the photos of the chapel?" she asked again.

"There are several photos of the chapel, from the front, sides and rear. There are a few pictures of the windows and the front door. There is another one showing what looks like a priest by a gate talking to another priest. The rest of the pictures seem to be of surrounding building and brush at the rear of the chapel." He waited to see if Loomis had other questions, and she did.

But, before she could speak he said, "I am holding a broacher of ATV models with a few circled. The other map appears to be with coordinates out in the desert of Afghanistan. No pictures to go along with that so it is your guess as to what it means."

"Thank you so much, sir. Your team up there has filled in a bunch of the puzzle we needed to fill for a successful prosecution. I look forward to getting the property from you once you process it. Thank you again." With that she hung up.

When she exited the bathroom, the unknown male that she left in the bed, had dressed and left the bedroom without even a thank you. This is how she liked it. Wham, bang, thank you mame.

He must have heard enough of the conversation, and even though it was one-sided, realized that she must have been a cop. She wondered what a background check on him might reveal.

CHAPTER 43

"Frank, can you hear me? Frank, can you hear me, over?" Joe repeated. The reception was not too bad, with only a little static. Nancy got to the walkie-talkie before Frank and said, "Yes, we hear you. Here's Frank." She handed it over to him.

"Frank here, go ahead."

"Frank, this is Jessie. We are now setting up base camp. We found a good place to hide the truck and the ATVs worked perfectly, No problems at this end. How about there? Over."

"Everything here is fine except for almost monsoon weather, over, "Frank replied.

"We will wait until you give us the green light, over," said Jessie.

Nancy, still with no clothes on, came up behind Frank and placed her nude, cool body against his back. "Ok, try to get some sleep. If this rain keeps up, you guys will hit the chapel tonight. I will give you plenty of notice, out," said Frank. "Copy," responded Jessie.

Frank turned as Nancy's body just glided from his back to his front. Frank framed her face with his hands and said, "You know, when this is over, I will have to make you an honest woman."

"Yeah," Nancy said. "Actions are stronger than words, Sarge," followed by grabbing his hands and kissing them softly.

"No, seriously, God damn it. Once we complete this mission and cash in, I want to take you to South Africa and buy you the biggest diamond I can find and get married. That is, if you will have me." Frank waited for her response.

Instead, Nancy, standing in front of Frank nude, began to cry.

"What, did I say something wrong?" Frank asked with sadness in his voice.

Nancy still did not respond, but shook her head side-to-side.

Then she said, "Frank, do you realize that all the time we have been together, you have never, even once, hinted about getting married. I never wanted to bring it up, since I thought that if I did, you would never want to see me again."

"But I said many times that I loved you," Frank said. "Yes, but by today's standards, that doesn't mean that those people in that relationship, would naturally get married.

"Gee Nancy, I am not good at this stuff. I hoped that you knew when I said I loved you, that this meant that I wanted to spend the rest of my life with you."

Nancy started to cry again. Frank sat down on the bed in a way that Nancy was standing in front of him. Frank placed his arms around her waist and pulled her nude body towards his face. He kissed her belly button and said, "Look, I would understand if you do not want to marry me. I'm a lot older than you and definitely not one of your scholar friends that you are surrounded with each day."

Nancy, wiping the tears away from under her eyes, said, "Shut up Frank. You are going to ruin this whole event. She pushed him back on the bed, climbed on top of him and said, "There is no other man in the world I want to marry more than you."

CHAPTER 44

Fattah and his team of 8 terrorists arrived at the hotel in Addis Ababa. He rented five rooms, placing two individuals to each room, and taking one room solely for himself so that, when he felt safe, he could sneak out and contact his handler. Two days earlier, he had briefed al-Otaibi, Khalimov and Yusaf of his plan for the raid on the chapel. The three terrorist leaders were impressed with the overall strategy Fattah explained and gave their blessing for its immediate execution. Airline tickets, passports, and visas were prepared for him and his team. Weapons would be waiting for them outside of Axum at a location only given to Fattah. He and his team would meet another brother in the jungle a kilometer outside of the town. Once armed, they would execute his plan. Now his team, secured in their rooms, waited for his command to start their jihadist activities.

At 2300 hours, feeling that his team was asleep, Fattah left his room quietly and proceeded to hail a cab. As was done previously, he had placed a phone call to his handler using another burn phone al-Otaibi had given him with the other documents needed for travel. He was to meet his new handler at an Internet cafe. Upon meeting him, Fattah told him of the plan he was to executed the next day. His handler seemed to be more interested in the fact that once again, all three terrorist leaders were still in the desert camp together.

Finally, after Fattah explained the plan he designed, his handler gave him a small tracking devise, instructing him to hide it in his clothing. This would help locate him and his team once they entered the jungle to meet up with the weapons supplier. After doing so, Fattah's handler told him that he would immediately notify the Agency and devise a counter plan for Fattah's assault strategy. Unfortunately, he would not be able to relay what that plan would be before Fattah's and his team had already begun operations.

CHAPTER 45

Fattah and his team began their trek in heavy rain, into the jungle outside of Axum at 0300 hours. They traveled to within one kilo meter of the city where they found a small encampment of what appeared to be pilgrims but Fattah knew why they were there. After exchanging brief greetings, the gun runners removed a large carpet which covered an earthen pit. There inside, Fattah and his team could see AK-47s and knives.

Fattah and his team members began inspecting the weapons trove when suddenly, a loud explosion and flash temporarily blinded and disoriented everyone in the encampment. Fattah quickly assessed what was happening and dropped to the ground. Sporadic gunfire erupted and he could hear several of his team members and others in the encampment scream out in pain.

From his position on the ground, Fattah saw several commando style individuals, wearing camouflage and black ski masks, run from the cover of the jungle foliage towards the interior of the camp. Everyone, including Fattah, were handcuffed with nylon cuffs. Those that were obviously dead, were also cuffed. Black bags that allowed for ventilation were placed on the heads of everyone. With military precision, the weapons were confiscated, still alive, were walked back deeper into the jungle to waiting military trucks for transportation. The dead were placed in several trucks along with some wounded or uninjured. The whole operation seemed to Fattah to take less than 5 minutes.

The trucks proceeded for several miles. The smells coming from the dead and injured permeated the interior of the truck containing Fattah. Fattah was hoping that this was an operation carried out by his CIA colleagues and not some Ethiopian drug lord. To Fattah, it would make no sense for a drug lord to cuff individuals, included the dead, and then place bags over their heads. They would have instead, killed everyone present and secure the weapons. He hoped he was correct.

CHAPTER 46

The trucks came to a stop in what seemed like an airport. This, Fattah judged, from the sound of at least one plane and the smell of aviation fuel. The individuals were ordered out of the trucks and told to stand where placed. Fattah did as instructed. He then heard the dragging of bodies of the dead and the transporting of the wounded, being removed from the trucks.

An order was given to those that could stand, to place their hand on the shoulder of a person next to them. They were aided by their captors. When Fattah reached out with his hand to touch a person he hoped was next to them, a hand reached out and slowly pulled him from the group.

The procession of men was escorted towards the sound of at least one plane. Fattah could hear them being assisted into the plane and eventually he heard at least two doors close.

The next sound was the acceleration of plane engines and the rapid sound of tires running along a runway.

He stood by himself, waiting for further instructions. Finally, a quick pull of the black bag that covered his head, allowed for blinding light to overtake his face. He raised his still cuffed hands to aid him is shading the sunlight, but then felt his hands being grabbed and the feel of a knife cutting off the plastic cuffs.

Being able to focus now, he saw the friendly face of his handler shouldering an assault rifle.

"You did good, my man. Really good," his handler said.

After shaking hands and getting oriented, Fattah saw that he was correct in his assessment. They were in a stretch of jungle in which an airfield had been created out of the jungle. He learned that it had been previously used by a drug lord and taken over by the CIA.

The dead had left in the first plane prior to the truck transporting Fattah arriving. He heard the departure of the second plane containing those that were wounded or captured. He was told that the dead would be photographed and fingerprinted for possible identification.

The two of them climbed into a Jeep and were driven a few miles to a temporary command center located under a thick jungle canopy of trees. Fattah counted approximately fifteen other males in the encampment and three women. All were dressed in similar camouflage as his handler.

Fattah was given a cold can of Coke which he quickly consumed. A submarine type sandwich was also given to him along with a bag of chips and another can of soda. He was left alone to eat his meal. He surveyed the command center and did not see any of his former team nor individuals who were with the gun runner.

"Fattah, come here. I think you will want to see this!" said his handler waving from a tent located in the center of the compound.

Fattah entered the tent which was dark inside except from the lamination coming from various computer screens and a large television screen approximately 10 feet long by 6 feet wide.

There, displayed on the screen, was an overhead shot of a location Fattah knew well. It was his former terrorist camp.

In the middle of the screen there was a large + that seemed to be manipulated over various tents. Fattah was asked which tent did he attend his meeting with al-Otaibi, Khalimov and Yusaf?

Fattah pointed in the direction of the tent in question and the large + moved over that location.

He was asked by a female at the controls that manipulated the sighting + if she was correct in identifying the target.

Fattah replied that this was the correct tent.

The female controller looked at who appeared to be her superior while placing her right index finger on a joy-stick trigger. Fattah saw the older male individual look at the female controller and heard him say, "Execute!"

With that command, the controller pulled the trigger and then said, "Boom"!

Within nanoseconds, a large blast of white light consumed the television screen. When the screen returned to its normal contrast, only an empty desert setting was seen. No tents, no animals, no humans – just a desolate stretch of sand from horizon to horizon.

Fattah eventually turned from the screen and looked at his handler.

"What now?" he asked.

"Now you will be reunited with your family and granted asylum in the United States," said his handler, at which point, those in the tent that heard the conversation, gave him an applause.

Chapter 47

As night approached, Frank and Nancy again ventured out of their hotel to have dinner. Still raining, still no guards.

They both ordered a traditional Ethiopian dish that consists of vegetables and often, like this time, very spicy meat. It came in the form of a thick stew, served on top of injera, a large sourdough flatbread. Nancy enjoyed the vegetables, but when no one was looking, scraped the spicy meat onto Frank's plate, who graciously loved it. They washed their meal down with tea and, besides staring at each other, said nothing as they digested their last meal in Ethiopia.

"So, Frank, how many kids shall we have?" she asked.

Before he could answer they heard a rumble sound like thunder coming towards the center of the square. Frank recognized immediately the sound of military vehicles. They both got up from their table and started for the exit door, while Frank, at the same time, left the money and tip.

They walked outside and saw in front of the chapel and adjacent church, two Jeeps with mounted fifty-caliber machineguns bolted to the floor in the middle of the vehicle. There were two other military type trucks. Frank did not see the truck Jessie had just driven, but if he had, he would say they were similar. Nancy showed no fear and stared at Frank. Frank grabbed her hand and they continued displaying the same behavior they had many times before, in hopes of not bringing attention to them.

Exiting the front Jeep was a tall Ethiopian male with a lot of scrambled eggs on the visor of his cap. Giving orders, he obviously was in charge and held rank. Canvas flaps in the back of the trucks opened and several, heavily armed soldiers climbed down. In total, Frank counted 29 men, but who were they, and why, on this time and day, were they here?

Shit, thought Frank. Ok Frank, think, prepare for the worst, so when it happens, you will not be surprised. But, surprised he was.

Frank and Nancy exchanged looks again, but did not say anything. They walked outside and joined maybe a dozen locals who also heard the noise of the approaching vehicles and needed to satisfy their curiosity. Holding hands, Nancy and Frank stood with the others even though they stood out of the crowd with their American clothing.

The rain continued to come down and the soldiers and their leader went into the same café that Nancy and Frank had just left. The crowd started to return for cover from the rain, so Nancy and Frank decided to walk back to their hotel. Once inside, Nancy recognized the front lobby employee, with whom she began a friendship with during their many prior trips. Although she spoke in broken English, Nancy believed she would know what it is happening.

"Gee, what is all the excitement outside?" Nancy asked, turning away from the female employee and staring outside with Frank.

"Oh, those are part of Ethiopian army. They come in here about every three months like on training. Sorry for my English." She blushed. "This has been going on for maybe thirty years," she said.

"Why," Nancy asked. Everything that was being said, Frank overheard. He acted as if he was more interested in the vehicles the soldiers arrived in.

"Well, for many years, very bad here. Genocide in Ethiopia resulted in civil war, like you had in the United States, yes?"

"Yes," Nancy said, "but ours did not last almost thirty years."

"I understand. It really started when my country had many famines, one right after another. This time was 1972 to 1973; long time ago. We had emperor then named Haile Selassie the 1st. He did, no good job. He said that no water was natural disaster and did not help my people so they became upset with his rule.

A new leader made a military junta. His name, Mengistu Haile Mariam. He staged a coup and Selaisse's assassination. We have a lot of assassination in our country. He no good either. Everything he did come at expense of us." She paused to see if Nancy was still interested, and she was.

"Go on," Nancy said. "This is really good research material that I could use in my book."

The front lobby female desk clerk got excited, thinking that there may be a chance for her name to appear in the book. She smiled and started off again, "The Dergue ruled for long time, maybe 20 years, under a violent regime of terror, torturing, imprisoning, and killing those who opposed them. Maybe tens of thousands of victims; young, old, babies. It did not matter your religion or race. If they thought you were not, how you say loyal?" She stopped to see if Nancy understood.

Nancy said yes and repeated the word, "loyal."

Now our government is much better. We still have times with no water, but the government helps when this happens. To make sure people are not trying to throw out new government like before, many armies like this, drive around our country to show that government is in charge." She stopped and looked at Nancy to see if she did a good job.

Before Nancy could say anything else, Frank asked, "How long do they stay in town?"

That sounded too suspicious to Nancy, so she added, "there are so many of them and the café they are in, the one my boyfriend and I go too always, is so small. I don't know where else we can go and get our meals."

She responded, "Do not worry, most of the time, after they eat and drink, they leave for the next town or city. I member them staying overnight one time, but that was a long time ago. You see, they go." She smiles, figuring she did a good job. Then she asked Nancy if she needed her name for the book.

Nancy, a little stunned, said, "Oh yes, could you please write it down on something for me?"

While this was happening, Frank was processing what the next course of action should be. If they decided to stay overnight, there is no way they can hit the church. And, if they do leave, will it allow enough time for the job? Do they ever double back?

CHAPTER 48

Back in their room, Nancy did not feel she needed to ask Frank a stupid question like, "what are we going to do?" She knew his mind was working overtime and felt that it was best to remain silent.

Finally, he looked at her and asked for the walkie-talkie. Nancy handed it to him.

Turning it on he said, "Hello, this is Frank, over." He repeated, "Hello, this is Frank, over."

Two clicks sounded on the walkie-talkie, and then a response. "Hello Frank, this is Joe, copy?"

"Joe, I copy. Are the rest of the guys close by to monitor, over?" Frank said.

"One minute Frank," Joe said. Apparently leaving the mic open, Frank and Nancy could hear Joe calling over Ed, Ruben and Jessie, followed by him saying, it's Frank.

"Frank," said Joe, "we are all here, go ahead."

"Ok guys, we have a problem here. A few minutes ago, about 30 soldiers in two trucks and two Jeeps, arrived in Axum.

"Fuck!" someone said, but Frank could not determine who said it.

Frank continued, "According to one of the locals, this means nothing since it happens about every two to three months; like a show of force so no one gets any ideas about overthrowing the government.

Nancy's source told us that the soldiers rarely stay overnight. That is the problem however, since we can't hit the chapel with them here, and we do not know when they will leave." Frank stopped to let his concerns sink in to all concerned.

"What do you want us to do Frank," asked Joe. "Well, there is only one thing we can do as I see it," Frank said. "Until these guys leave, stay at the base camp on standby. If they leave tonight and we have enough time to execute the plan, I will give you the all clear sign. Beyond that, there is nothing we can do, copy?"

"We copy Frank and will be standing by, out." With that, it became a hurry up and wait game.

Frank stood by the window overlooking the last truck that arrived, hoping to see troops climb back inside soon. For now, however, there was no activity by any of the vehicles. The soldiers, like the locals, do not want to stand out in the rain either.

Frank continued to evaluate the situation as it stood. His plan called for no weapons other than a personal knife unless they absolutely needed to take someone out. Each of his team members were well versed in hand-to-hand combat. Everything else his group had, fit into their cover story; filthy rich Americans, with a yacht, beautiful ladies, money being thrown around, even having them purchase of fishing gear, all part of the plausibility for being in the region. There is no way his group could handle thirty soldiers, no matter how poorly trained they may be. No, Frank thought, they had to wait it out. He just hoped that the weather would continue to be miserable.

CHAPTER 49

Frank and Nancy gave up watching out the window for any movement down below. They both figured that if any of those military vehicles started up, especially the trucks, they would hear them. Instead they lay on the bed in their normal, relaxing lying position, with Nancy in Frank's arms. This time however, neither of them had sex on their mind. Nancy also decided that it was not the right time to return to the subject matter at the restaurant, that had been interrupted when the soldiers arrived.

At approximately 10:45, there was the loud rumbling sound again, the sound they had heard earlier. Both Nancy and Frank sprang to the window and saw soldiers climbing up into the trucks. The Jeep's drivers also fired up their engines. They then saw the ranking officer walking out of the café with no one else following. He was the last to exit. He climbed into his Jeep and waving with his right hand, signaling to the convoy to get moving, and off they went.

Frank looked at his watch again; plenty of time he thought as he looked at Nancy. She nodded.

A quick assessment of the weather, the surrounding area of the chapel and church, no locals about, no volunteer guards. More rain and now thunder and lightning. Time to execute the plan.

"This is Frank, do you copy?" he said into the walkie-talkie.

"We are here Frank, go ahead," someone said at the other end. The rain was really coming down and now thunder and lightning were making their appearance at their base camp.

"You have a green light, I repeat, green light," Frank said.

"We copy, out," was the response.

Frank looked at this watch again while his mind raced. Nancy felt a sense of not only anticipation, but stress and concern invading her body. Most of her academic life was in the research of Biblical truths: to research exactly how accurate the Bible accounts were. She did not tell James, but when he made his reference to the famous movie, Indiana Jones and Raiders of the Lost Ark at the bar, she too, had become fascinated with the whole Ark thing when she saw the film. Did it really exist and if so, where could it be? All her research said it was here, just a few blocks away. Was it really coated with pure gold and what really was inside? Would they find Aaron's rod, or maybe even Moses's rod, who knows? All that other nonsense shown in the film when the Nazis opened it on that island was just Hollywood. But a few hours from now, if the Ark of the Covenant was indeed inside that chapel, she would be recognized by her peers worldwide and be on top of everyone's list as the greatest Biblical Historian and Archeologist of the 21st century. She didn't care as much about the money. Prestige was what she wanted. She didn't want to spend the rest of her life with Frank or James. They were just useful puppets to get the Ark. If they did receive millions of dollars as their share for finding the Ark, she would not have to worry about him or James. She would just grab the Ark, her share of the money, and disappear.

Frank noticed that Nancy appeared to be in deep thought. He asked her if she was ok. She did not respond, so Frank asked again.

"Nancy, are you ok?"

Finally, Nancy heard his question and she "woke up" from her thoughts. "Yes babe, I'm fine, just anxious. "What time do you think the guys will arrive?" she asked.

Out of habit, Frank looked at his watch and said, "Unless they reach a washout or something that would slow them down, I think they should be here in thirty." They continued their wait.

CHAPTER 50

The walkie – talkie cracked and Frank and Nancy heard, "Frank, this is Jessie, do you read."

"We read you Jessie. What's your location?" Frank asked.

"We are in the bushes behind the chapel. Is it clear to execute?"

Frank looked deeply into Nancy's eyes. She nodded, indicating, let's do this.

Frank spoke into the walkie-talkie and said that everything was clear and told them to switch over to their normal communication system."

Jessie acknowledged the command and dumped the walkie-talkie into a pile of rubble and switched over to the communication system they had used on all their black ops assignments. Joe, Ruben and Ed followed his lead, putting their microphone in front of their face.

Frank, called to the team with his communication set, "Acknowledge that system is working. Jessie?"

Jessie acknowledged.

"Joe?"

Joe acknowledged. "Ed?"

Ed acknowledged. "Ruben?"

Ruben acknowledged.

Ed motioned to the other three, that he was going to cut the phone line that Nancy and Frank had spotted. Once he cut the line, Ed turned on the cellphone jammer. The only communications that would work now was theirs.

Ed went back to the rear of the chapel and rejoined with Ruben, Jessie and Joe.

Frank gave a long kiss and hug to Nancy and left her for his position at street level to take out anyone who started to interfere with the operation. He held his Mk-3 knife in his right hand with the blade against the inside of his arm. No one was seen on the street. The thunder and lightning only seemed to increase when he stood on the sidewalk across from the chapel and church. Good, he thought, the more noise, the better.

The four Banshees approached the fencing at the rear of the chapel. Lightning flashes made their infra-red goggles useless until they got into the chapel. The fence consisted of some very cheap wrought iron, and it was attached to thicker wrought iron poles in 10' sections. With the noise from the rain, thunder and lightning, they took out the noise reduction grinder and easily cut the two nuts and bolts holding each section to their poles attached at a welded L shaped connection. That way, they could remove the section of fencing, get inside the perimeter, and then place the section of fencing back on the L shaped welded connection.

In less than five minutes, the 10' section of fencing had been removed and replaced after the four of them entered the perimeter. They quickly approached the left rear portion of the wall, at which time Jessie told Ed to use the Range-R and go to the side of the chapel and see how many people were inside.

Ed pulled at the Range-R from the pouch he had tied to his pants belt and positioned himself about halfway down the right-side wall. Turning it on, he scanned the chapel from the front to rear. He saw a figure laying down, probably on a bed. No one else was visible. He thought, that must be the guardian.

"I see one person laying down on something. No one else seen and no other movement, so I guess there is no dog or cat." Ed said.

"Copy that," Jessie said. "Stay at your position and monitor any movement."

With that said, Joe pulled out a heavy-duty glass cutter with a circular suction cup. He placed it on the small square pane of glass in the lower section of the window. The wind, as well as the thunder and lightning picked up. There would be no way anyone inside the chapel could hear their activity.

It was very easy to remove a 1" circular section from the glass. Once this was completed, Jessie motioned to Joe who handed him a hose attached to one of two gas canisters. He also handed him a rag. With the gas canisters on the ground below the window and the nub of the hose inserted into the interior of the chapel, Jessie nodded to Joe, to turn on the gas. Jessie could hear the hissing of the gas as it entered the chapel. He secured the rag on the outside of the hose to create a seal.

"Frank, we are filling the chapel with Special K."
"Roger that," Frank responded.

"Still clear outside?" asked Jessie.

Frank gave the area a once over again and said, "All clear, proceed."

After the first canister emptied, Joe quickly connected the hose to the second and the process continued. They had determined that with the estimated size of the interior of the chapel, that they should use both canisters just to be safe. Finally, the second canister emptied. They left the hose inserted in the window pane with the rag.

"Frank, both canisters have been deployed," said Joe. Frank acknowledged his transmission.

"Ed, we are coming towards you," Joe said. "Copy that," Ed responded.

After meeting up again with Ed, the four of them moved to the far corner of the chapel adjacent to the front. Joe quickly looked around the corner and saw that it was clear. More cracks of lightning and thunder. The rain continued to pour and flooded the area.

Using what they considered the smallest amount of C-4 explosive they felt would do the job of blasting the hinges on one side of the two front doors, Joe applied the substance and timer. Before setting it to go off, he called to Frank.

"Frank, we are ready to blast the door," he said.

Frank searched the streets for any movement. He checked to see if any new lights had come on in another of the surroundings. He asked Nancy up above, if she saw anything. She searched back and forth on the streets and saw that no one was venturing outside.

"All clear from here, Frank," she said.

Frank said, "All clear from all positions. Execute."

CHAPTER 51

Joe set the timer and the four went around the far corner of the chapel. It was perfect timing, for the blast sound was eliminated by one of the loudest thunder blast of the evening. The door just stood there. Initially the four thought that maybe they did not use enough C-4. Jessie however, grabbed the door handle on the side where the explosive had been detonated, and pulling on it, the door gave way. They were now ready to enter.

After putting on gas masks, they put their helmets back on and pulled down their night vision goggles. Frank and Nancy, from their position above and at street level, were only able to see partial movement of the four, almost as if a strobe light, being made by the lightning, was illuminating their action.

Once inside, the four took time to oriented themselves as to the furniture inside, as well as to find and check on the welfare of the guardian. The only illumination inside the chapel were several candles burning. The guardian was easy to spot, laying on a bed no wider that a child's bunk bed. Ed checked his pulse and he was breathing. He gave the rest of the Banshees a thumbs up.

For some reason, they had expected the gas to dissipate once it had been introduced into the chapel, but instead, it seemed to turn into a mist. No, not a mist, more like a thick fog and it was getting thicker. "What the hell," Jessie said. In all their black op missions where they used this same type of gas, they never saw it build up on the ground and have a mist-like appearance.

Neither Frank, nor Nancy heard his transmission and assumed that things were going as planned. They continued to check the streets and buildings; still all clear.

Frank decided to break the silence and said, "report." There was no response, so Frank ordered again, "report." Still nothing. "Nancy, are you monitoring anything from them?" he asked.

Nancy answered with a "no." Then she said, "maybe there is something wrong with either their equipment or ours.

"Can't be, you can hear me," Frank said. Frank told Nancy that he was going to get closer to the chapel and see what he could learn. Nancy said, "copy." Frank left the cover of his position and started to walk towards the main church instead of the chapel in case someone was watching him. He did not want to bring attention to the main object of the operation.

Looking around inside of the chapel, the four saw only evidence of a Spartan lifestyle by the guardian. There was a table, a radio, a refrigerator, a small two burner stove, no television, and no computer. They found a small bathroom with a toilet, washbasin and shower. There was also a stackable washer and dryer unit. They saw more candles which, although burning, had pretty much run their course for the evening. They started to walk forward, spread out almost from wall to wall.

The mist or fog was getting thicker and they determined that it was actually coming from the back of the chapel near the area that they had inserted the gas hose. Lightning strikes still occasionally caused havoc to their infra-red equipment but without it, they could not move freely in the room. The did not bring flashlights because someone outside of the chapel might notice their use and become suspicious.

As they started toward the back of the chapel where the fog was coming from, they saw that there was a second room, breaking up the main chapel area that was occupied by the guardian. This room also had a door, but different than the main exterior door they blew. This door was a single vs. double door and appeared to have gold overlay applied to the wooden surface. The mist was coming from under this door and seemed to be pulsating. Strange, they all thought, but this must be it. This is where the Ark was kept. They could "smell it."

"Frank, this is Joe. We have found another smaller room inside the chapel. It is located near the rear where we pumped in the gas. Do you copy?"

No response.

"Frank, Nancy, do either of you copy? Joe said. No response.

"You guys copy?" he asked the other three. They all gave thumbs up indicating that they could.

"What the fuck," asked Joe.

"Don't worry about it," said Jessie. "It's probably the fucking storm. Let's breach the door, grab the damn Ark, and get out of here. I got a lady waiting for me." The others laughed.

CHAPTER 52

"God, damn it, will someone tell me what the hell is going on inside," said Frank. No response.

"Nancy, anything?" Frank asked. "Still nothing," she said.

Nancy could no longer see Frank from their room, even when lightning lit up the sky. The last time she saw him, he was walking towards the back of the chapel, then she lost him. The rain continued to come down and the street below her position was starting to look more like a pond, than a street that people traveled on.

Frank was beginning to have a hard time staying upright in his path to the rear wall of the chapel. Footing was now becoming traitorous. He had already done the splits a few times and had to use his hands, which he placed in the mud and water, to remain in an upright positon. Frank thought the something must be slowing the guys down, or the electricity from the storm or something inside the chapel, was messing around with their communication gear. They should have already secured the Ark, he thought, and made it out of the church, back to their hidden ATVs. Hell, maybe they were already enroute back to the base camp, so excited the assholes forgot to tell him and Nancy. Still, only being a few feet from the wall and the cut portion of the window, he heard nothing. He could see the gas canisters, with a hose from one of them running up to the window and still hanging, being wedged in place by a piece of rag. He trained his team well, he thought.

Frank started to walk along the side of the chapel towards the front door. Maybe someone got hurt inside. Shit, he thought, a lot could be going on inside, he had to check it out, for his own damn curiosity and for the sake of his Banshee team. Panic set in as Frank could no longer lift his legs.

The ground was sucking him deeper and deeper. This could not be happening he thought. He tried to pull his legs up, one at a time, but instead he was sinking deeper into the mud and rain. The water and mud had now reached his waist, but this could not be since he could see the ground around him, still with patches of vegetation. Did he, by chance, step into a crevice that had been covered over with water and mud? What other explanation could explain the dangerous situation he found himself in. "Son-of-a-bitch, what the fuck is happening? God, damn it, I need help out here. Can anyone hear me?"

"Hey guys, I need help now. I mean now! I am outside the rear wall, hurry!" he shouted. No one responded to his call for aid.

"Nancy, can you read me? I am trapped in a hole and being dragged down. Can you try to reach the guys, quickly please!" Frank pleaded. No one responded.

More thunder and lightning and a heavier downpour of rain. Frank hoped that by not struggling, he would not continue his descent into the watery grave that awaited. But it was no use; the water had now reached his chin and deeper he went. Flapping his arms and trying to tread water did not help. Screaming for help did not bring anyone. Finally, Frank felt as if someone or something grabbed his legs and pulled him under. All that remained was a few air bubbles that made it to the surface. Frank was gone.

CHAPTER 53

From her upstairs room, Nancy continued to use the lightning flashes to see any movement down below. She saw nothing. Communications were not working and she felt blind, deaf and helpless. The hell with it, she thought, as she grabbed her jacket and headed down the stairs to street level. She would explain to Frank later, why she gave up her position. She needed to know what was happening. After all, it was her and Frank's plan.

Once she made it outside of the hotel, a lightning bolt struck a tree near the main church splitting it in two. The fire that it created, was put out almost instantly by the heavy rain. A light came on at the main church so Nancy retreated to the façade of the hotel and tried to use it as cover. Whoever turned on the light, must have been awakened by the tree spitting in two. Satisfied that this was the cause of the noise; the light was turned off and no one came outside. Nancy still decided to wait a few minutes. Maybe the person who turned on the light was getting a jacket, or flashlight, and was preparing to come outside for a more detailed investigation. She did not want to get caught in the middle of the street, halfway to the chapel.

Jessie told Ed to place a small amount of C-4 near the door handle; just enough to break the locking mechanism. Joe thought they should try something else because he did not want to leave any gold behind that was embedded in the wooden door. Jessie told him that any gold that came off the door due to the blast was all his. Satisfied, Joe, Ed, Ruben and Jessie moved several yards back. Ed set off the timer. The door swung open and then they saw it; just as Nancy had shown them in her slide presentation.

The Ark of the Covenant was on a platform, almost like an altar. When the lightning flashes illuminated the room, the mist, coming from beneath the Ark, turned to a golden hue. It was very beautiful they all thought. They all noticed that poles were already inserted into the golden rings on all four corners. There would be no need for the telescopic poles they had in their leg pockets. So transfixed to the golden hue in the room, none of them really noticed that the mist was emanating from below the Ark. It was not a concentration of Special K gas that they had pumped into the chapel.

The fog or mist, or whatever it was, started to swirl and rose to their waist level. The Ark began to glow, followed by a high piercing sound. The sound got higher and higher. The four of them removed their helmets so that they could place their hands on over their ears; anything to try and muffle the terrible sounds.

As the thunder and lightning increased outside, the flashes allowed them to see movement from the base of the Ark. Movement that they determined were serpents, serpents slithering out from beneath the Ark and disappearing into the mist.

"What the fuck?" called out Ruben." He grabbed for his knife, but it fell into the mist that was getting not only thicker, but began to pulse, rising and falling a foot or so. It was as if someone or something was inhaling, taking in the mist, and then exhaling. Ruben reached into the mist searching for his knife. He felt the first bite on his right hand and quickly pulled up his hand. Attached to it and trying to encircle Ruben's arm, was a large snake whose fangs were chewing away flesh. Ruben try to shake the snake free, but it only seemed to make it more aggressive. He felt more bites on both of his legs. He could not stand and fell to his knees into the mist. The other three, witnessing only part of this due to the darkness, could not help. Ruben, was gone.

Instead of the room being illuminated by sporadic lightning strikes, light was coming from under the lid of the Ark. Yes, the Ark's lid had somehow slide open a short distance and light, getting brighter and brighter, took over the room. It had a strobe-like pattern to it, making the surrounding area and the three of them, seem to move in slow motion. The light reached an intense level that none of them could tolerate. They had to make a choice of protecting their ears, or be blinded by the light.

Ed started to retreat and could feel movement both under and on top his feet. He stepped on a few and began to slip on the residue of their squashed bodies. He began to fall so he reached out to a bookcase near the wall. As soon as he placed his left hand on the bookcase, a large snake bit him. The pain was excruciating and through the pulsating light, he saw a second and then a third snake bite the same hand before he could extract it. But it was more than snake bites, these snakes were taking chucks of his flesh as they shook back and forth, still attached to his hand. He began to scream, but the others had their own problems to deal with.

Joe could feel a snake crawl up his pants leg. He tried to reach down into the mist or whatever it was, and tried to find where the snake's head was, to pull it off. By doing so, he felt the first of many bites to his lower and upper legs. He felt blood running down his pant legs on the inside. He legs became numb from the venom. He screamed, but it was lost in the harsh squeal from the Ark. He fell into the mist and immediately received snake bites to his chest, arms, neck and cheek. He could taste the venom enter his throat. He knew he was through.

Jessie could not see any of the other Banshees. Either they somehow made it out of the chapel, or they were dead. Kicking the snakes that he could feel were trying to attach themselves to his legs, he felt a few bites, but due to his size, the venom so far, did not affect him. He backed himself into a corner to the left of the Ark. The Ark's lid slid a little more and the light that was coming from it, now turned blood red. The light seemed to now pull up some of the mist which rose to the height of the ceiling. It was like some of the ancient drawings Nancy showed the group when she discussed the "power" of the Ark.

Something was happening to his skin, both on his hands and face and rest of his body. He looked down at his right hand and using lightning strikes for greater illumination, saw boils throbbing and erupting with pus, having an acid type effect on the skin adjacent to the boils. More and more boils appeared on his hands and he could feel that they were spreading, everywhere. His face was now covered. He continued to receive more and more strikes from the snakes, but the pain of the boils was much more intense, causing him to fall to his knees.

Now his eyes began to protrude from their sockets. He vision was lost. Blood poured from his ears, mouth, and eyes. He reached up for his left ear to try and stop the bleeding, but his ears began to curl inward, inward back into his head until they were gone, and so was Jessie, who fell into the mist.

The lid of the Ark sealed itself. The horrible debilitating sound stopped. The mist faded away.

CHAPTER 54

Nancy, feeling it was now safe, left the side of the hotel and walked in the direction of the main church. Reaching it, she saw no one up and about, so she felt it was now safe to go to the back of the chapel. There she thought, she would see Frank, and the guys and understand what was taking so long.

Something caught her eye. Even as the rain continued to pour, the lightning strikes lit up the area and ricocheted off the rain water that continued to accumulate on the ground around the chapel. Whatever it was seemed to sparkle. Could the guys have found diamonds or other jewels in the chapel? Maybe all the historians were wrong and inside the Ark of the Covenant there really was valuables such as precious gems and gold coins. Perhaps some of the loot fell out of the Ark when the guys were transporting it back to their ATVs. Maybe Frank caught up with them and was helping them get the Ark to the ATVs because it was so heavy with gold.

Another lightning strike showed her what was on the ground sparkling. It can't be, she thought. Darkness returned. She would have to wait for another strike. She reached down and waited. Another lightning strike lit up the ground and there is was. She quickly grabbed it and stood up. It was Frank's Saint Michael's medal that his mother had given him.

As loudly as she thought was safe, she called out his name. No response. She put the medal in her pocket and would give it to him when she saw him. He will be so relieved when he gets his medal back, she thought. She continued to the back of the chapel, still making sure she had not gotten any one's attention. She saw no one. The section of fencing removed by the guys, was standing open by itself allowing enough space for her to enter. That's weird, she thought. She could have sworn that she heard Frank tell them to put it back in place after they entered the courtyard, and again, after they left. They must still be inside the chapel, she thought. She knew this was not part of Frank's plan, but she was dying to get a glimpse of what the interior of the chapel that held the Ark of the Covenant looked like. She envisioned grabbing the attention of people who would be flocking to attend her lectures about the finding of the Ark of the Covenant. They would hang on her every word when she "took" them with her, inside the mysterious chapel.

She turned sideways and made her way past the fencing and walked to the far corner of the back wall and looked at the glass pane. There was no hole, nor any equipment laying at the base of the wall. What is going on she questioned herself. The only way to get answers was to make sure it was safe, and then enter the chapel from the front.

Working her way around to the front, she strained to hear above the thunder and lightning, any sounds from the inside. Still, she heard nothing. She reached the front door and found it closed, but unlocked. There were no signs of explosives being used. She had absolutely no military training, but had seen enough movies to know that when a door is exploded, there should be signs showing. Who knows, she thought, maybe the guardian never locked the doors, feeling secure with the wrought iron fencing. She opened the door and entered, calling out for Frank. He did not respond.

She waited a few seconds, inhaling the air from the chapel, to see if she would have any reaction, indicating that there was still gas present. She did not react to any possible residual remains of the gas, so she walked forward, still using the lightning flashes for illumination. She saw no one. She called out everyone's, "Frank, Jessie, Joe, Ruben, Ed. Come on guys, say something," She called out. Nothing.

A lightning strike allowed her to see the guardian laying on a small bed. He was still out, so the gas did its job. Oh God, she thought, I hope they did not use too much and kill him. She got closer to him and could hear breathing. She felt relieved.

She walked forward and saw another door at the far end of the chapel, highly decorated in what appeared to be gold. This is it, she thought. This is where the Ark was stored. But again, she noticed that there were no signs of forced entry into this interior room. She grabbed the heavy door and found it unlocked. She pulled the door open, still calling out Frank's name.

There it was, on what appeared to be an altar. It was just as she had imagined. The gold lid with the cherubs pointing at each other, just like the pictures she had seen in many biblical drawings. The poles, used for carrying the Ark, were already in place; but no one else was in the room. Where were they, she thought.

Maybe the Ark was too heavy. Maybe they went outside into the bushes or even the base camp to figure out how to move it. I sure hope we have enough time before daybreak to get the Ark out of here. She forgot about not finding a hole in the window pane, nor any equipment beneath the window. She was more interested in the find of the centuries, yes centuries. Her status in the academic world was secure for her lifetime and beyond. History books and archeology books will refer to her brilliance. She and Frank will be touring the world, conducting lectures about the find. Her thoughts did not consider that she, like the others, were thieves, and no one, outside of their little circle, would ever know who had stolen the Ark.

She walked forward towards the Ark. She would wait here until Frank and the others returned. She placed her hands on the gold overlay of the lid while continuing to walk around it. With her fingers, she explored the fine detail of cherubs. Frank and the guys would surely not object to her opening the Ark and seeing what is inside. Maybe they had already done so and found so much riches, that they had to go to the base camp. That was probably it she thought. After all, it was she, and she alone, whose research brought them to this spot, this discovery of all discoveries.

She again, approached the Ark, and with ease, slid the lid back just far enough without it sliding off onto the ground. A red mist started to stir inside and she became scared and backed away, but the mist continued to cascade from the Ark enveloping first her feet and then legs as it rose to her waist. She began to feel total relaxation of her whole body. It was like an endorphin rush. Her skin felt radiant and she felt so alive. She began to experience a sexual release that she achieved with Frank when they had great intercourse. Why was she so frightened, she asked herself? She again approached the Ark and looked inside. A light, almost the size of a pin head, began pulsating from the center of the mist. It grew bigger in size, but instead of illuminating the room, the glow rose straight up to the ceiling of the chapel.

She noticed movement from under that Ark.

Again, using the lightning as a source for illumination, she focused her vision in that area. First one, then thousands of beetles began almost floating to the ground encircling her feet. She screamed, but even more came out. Then, almost as suddenly as they appeared, they disappeared.

She then saw more movement. This time, whatever it was, was larger than the beetles. Then she saw them. Rats, thousands of rats, racing from the Ark onto the floor, scurrying to different parts of the interior room. Nancy quickly back up into the darkness, using her hands to find a wall, anything that she could use to avoid their advance. Then, like the beetles, they too disappeared. What was going on she thought. Maybe this happened to the Frank and the guys, and they freaked out and left.

No, that would never happen. These guys had already gone through hell and back many times. Beetles and rats would not scare them at all.

The light, still coming from the Ark, began to turn, slowly at first, and then with more velocity. Before long, it had almost hurricane speed, but the air was not moving around Nancy. Strange she thought. She should have been blown to the four walls of the chapel, and the sparse furnishings in the room should also have be affected.

Having no more fear, she became fascinated with the light. She then began having flashbacks of ancient pictures she had seen, showing the power of the Ark. About light and heat emanating from it. That's it, she thought. The Ark is happy to see me. Someone so brilliant, so worthy, that it is showing off its power.

How fortunate she was, she thought. The Ark truly belonged to her, and her alone.

"Show me more," she shouted. More thunder and lightning lite up the interior of the chapel.

Snakes, vipers, scorpions and started to appear from the Ark. Some coming from the bottom, some slithering or crawling out of the Ark itself. They advanced on her legs, but she got over her initial panic. This was another sign that she should possess the Ark, she believed. The snakes began wrapping around her legs. The scorpions climbed up on her also but did not seem to be in competition to the serpents. She received no bites or stings. And then, they too, disappeared. Only the light from the Ark remained.

Nancy reached into the swirling light. She placed her right hand inside first. It felt so warm and comforting on her hand that she placed her left hand inside also. She felt that her hands, hell her whole body, was being rejuvenated. Then, just as suddenly as the beetles, rats, snakes and scorpions appeared, something unseen force, grabbed her hands and began to pull her closer to the Ark, into the light. Nancy screamed, but no one responded. Where was Frank? Where were the other guys?

She began to feel an intense burning sensation in her pocket where she had placed Frank's medal. She wanted to reach in and pull out the medal that was burning her leg, causing excruciating pain. But the force grew and would not allow her to retrieve either of her hands. She could no longer see her arms, for the light had enveloped them.

Nancy felt herself being pulled up in the air. Yes, she knew she was off the ground. How could this be? She tried, with all her might, to pull her arms back, but now the wind, being generated from the light, was turning her around and around.

When will this show of power end, she thought. She had seen enough to realize now that the Ark of the Covenant, truly possessed powers that mankind could not fathom.

A horrific squeal emanated from the Ark. How she wanted to put her hands over her ears. She fought, but to no avail. She screamed as loud as she could. Around and around she went. She became dizzy. She vomited. Finally, the light and whirlwind had her. She was gone; absorbed by the wind and the light. It was over.

The wailing sound stopped. The light traveled back into the Ark. The lid slide back into place.

CHAPTER 55

Sunlight began to fill James' stateroom. When it hit his face, he woke up, and seeing that Danica, Agnetha and Monique were spread out on his bed, he got a huge smile, remembering his promise to the guys, that he would take good care of their ladies. The way they were sleeping, apparently, he had.

Checking his watch, he contacted Bashir and was surprised to learn that none of the guys had made it back yet. He really wanted to see their faces when they arrived and saw him surrounded with "their" ladies, nude, spread out on his bed.

He picked up his burner phone and called Frank. The phone rang but no one answered. Maybe Frank and Nancy were getting it on he thought, and they did not want to be disturbed.

Next, he called each of the guys by name. Again, no response. Hum, he thought, maybe they are out of range. Oh well, breakfast time. He had used a lot of energy last night, and who knows, if the guys get hung up, he may have to spend more energy with "their" ladies later.

The ladies joined him for breakfast and realizing the Frank wanted him to keep up with the charade of being a filthy rich American, he needed to "play" with the girls in the sea. So, he instructed his Bashir to take the yacht out for a day of cruising and fun in the sun. When he received notice from the guys that they were ready for extraction, they would quickly turn the yacht around.

While they cruised around, they stopped occasionally to use the water toys. At lunchtime, James tried to call Frank again. Still, no answer. He tried the guys. No answer. Something is not right he thought, but what was he to do? His responsibility was to drive the yacht around, show off his rich lifestyle, and wait for the guys to be picked up from the beach.

The package would then be secured onboard the yacht, and they would motor back to the marina. They were to stay another night, and then each of them were to leave. One of them would take the package. The job was almost done. Oh well, he thought, maybe they hit a snag. He could think of worse things to do than be surrounded by such lovely ladies, who, currently, he did not have to share.

They found a quiet cove and he instructed that the yacht drop anchor for a few hours. He gave permission to Bashir to take a much-deserved break, feeling that with the sea around the cove being so smooth, no one needed to be on anchor watch, or at the helm for that matter.

The ladies, spent from a day of frolicking in the sun and sea, asked James to come with them to his stateroom so that they could all take a nap, or, as Monique said, "whatever else they would think of," followed by giggles from Agnetha and Danica.

James was game. Why not? Once the other four returned, he would probably be the odd man out again. The crack in the fiberglass hull started in the engine room. The yacht began taking on hundreds of gallons of sea water. The alarm in the command bridge that would alert if the yacht was listing, did not activate, and even if it did, no one was there to hear it.

James and the girls heard a crash in his stateroom, waking them all up. An unknown object had slide onto the floor. He realized immediately that the stern of the vessel was listing badly. Something was dragging down that portion of the boat. Monique was the first to scream and start for the door. James told them not to panic and that he would go to the command bridge and see what was happening. When he opened the door, flames rushed into the room. All the girls were now screaming and panic spread among them. James pulled the comforter from the bed and covered the girls with it. It provided little resistance to the advancing flames. Smoke filled the stateroom. Breathing was becoming labored. Soon, everyone, including James, was unconscious. Soon they would be dead.

Bashir, so exhausted from fulfilling all his duties, did not wake from the listing of the yacht. It was not until he felt the sea water on his body that he woke and instantly panicked. But it was too late for him or the other crewmembers to save themselves. They, like the yacht, were swallowed up by the sea.

CHAPTER 56

Morning also broke inside the Axum chapel, waking the guardian. He stretched and rolled out of his bunk-size bed into a sitting position. He rose and walked to the small stove and turned on the fire, while placing his tea pot on the flame. He began eating breakfast and turned on the radio. He heard the bell ring outside near the wrought iron gate indicating that something had been left for him.

He unlocked the double doors and walked outside into the sunlight. The ground was damp, but the skies were clear. It will be a nice day in Axum, he thought. He walked to the gate, finding a basket of grocery items that he needed for the coming week. He unlocked the gate, picked up the basket and while walking back to the front of the church, decided to walk around the chapel. He placed the grocery items near the front door and started his walk. First down the side of the chapel nearest the main church, then around the back. Finally, he walked past the side that faced the hotel. Finding nothing amiss, he returned to the chapel, shut and locked the door. Another day of solitude.

Nancy's friend, the front lobby employee, wondered why she did not see either of her two favorite guests this morning. Normally they came bouncing down stairs with smiles on their faces, gave her a greeting, and then headed down the street to the café. Oh well, she thought, they seem like they can never keep their hands off each other, maybe they decided to make love this morning and stay in bed. Or, perhaps they left early, before she started her shift, to explore the countryside. She would see them later.

By late afternoon however, nearing the end of her shift, she decided to check on their welfare and see if they needed anything. With these friendlier gestures, she thought, the better chance of getting her name in Nancy's book.

She knocked on the door but there was no answer, nor any movement. She called out Nancy's name. Still no reply. Using her pass key, she opened the door to their room slightly, calling out Nancy's name again. She did not want to walk in while they were in a moment of passion. Still no one responded, so she walked in further. To her amazement, the bed was made, and all their luggage was gone. The room was spotless as if housekeeping had just made up their room.

She called housekeeping and asked when did they make up room 216? The woman who answered the phone, said that they had not made up the rooms on the second floor yet. She called her relief at the front desk, who normally comes to work early, and asked him, if by chance the guests of room 216 left during his shift last night. He could not recall who the guests were associated to that room, so she had to remind him, by describing Nancy. No male could forget seeing Nancy.

"No," he said, "he had no guest arrive or leave last night.'

This made no sense. They were not the type to skip out from paying for the use of their hotel room. In fact, on all their previous stays, they left a very nice tip to her and the hotel. She searched the room again, and could not find any trace of anyone being in this room for any length of time.

Chapter 57

One day later, some kids were playing hide-and-seek behind the back of the chapel; outside the fence of the courtyard. One of them went deep into the underbrush to hide and found four new ATVs, covered by some type of cloth that looked like leaves. No one else was around. He did not see anything inside the vehicles but he became scared and figured that he had better get out of the area because it might belong to the army.

He waited a day and curiosity got to him. He finally told his friends of his find a few days earlier. They all wanted to see, so they followed him into the underbrush where he last saw the ATVs. There they were, just like before. Still covered and still with no one around. He told his father who felt that he needed to call the army.

The next day, the same army unit that had patrolled the area a few nights ago in the storm, arrived and checked out the ATVs. The soldiers searched the surrounding area, but came up empty.

A detailed search was ordered around the outside of the chapel and adjacent church. Nothing was found at either location. They confiscated the ATVs. Not having a truck large enough at the time, four of the soldiers lucked out and got to drive them off.

CHAPTER 58

Nancy's friend, the hotel's front desk personnel, was still puzzled and disappointed at the sudden departure of her two favorite guests. She sure hoped that Nancy would include her name in her future book about Axum, the Ark of the Covenant, and how professional and helpful she had been to them on their many trips to her country.

On the hotel lobby counter were guest newspapers. She picked one up and glanced at the headlines and everything else on the front page. She saw one article about a super yacht missing for several days. Apparently, the article read, it belonged to a bunch of wealthy Americans and their lady friends, who had been partying around with them, starting in Saudi Arabia. No sighting of the ship has occurred for over a week now. A tragic fishing trip.

Another article was about a miracle appearing in a place called Tucson, Arizona. Some dirt bike riders found a building alone, in the middle of the desert. Authorities had no idea what it was, nor who build it. They placed pictures in various media outlets and started to receive calls from people stating that it is almost an identical rendition of the chapel in Ethiopia that supposedly contained the Ark of the Covenant.

As soon as this news got out, Tucson began receiving thousands of tourists and Christian pilgrims, flocking to this area of Arizona, to see this miracle first hand and worship it. Weird she thought. Could Nancy and Frank have learned about this, and that is why they left so soon, she asked herself.

She turned on the radio just to hear background noise as she works. She heard about an outbreak of the plague killing several rich Middle Easterners and their immediate family members. The expert being interviewed said that medical experts were perplexed that this type of plague had not been seen in decades, and that the symptoms displayed by the afflicted, were like those described in the Bible. Boils, blisters, horrible smell, and bites, covered their bodies.

The expert went on to say, that what was surprising to the CDC, was that the plague did not spread to others living nearby or having close contact with the dead. It was contained to a very small group, seemingly having no contact with rats or fleas, the common carriers associated with it.

CHAPTER 59

"Agent Loomis, can I help you?" said Loomis as she answered the phone call forwarded to her.

"Agent Loomis, this is Delaney. I am afraid that I have some bad news to share with you."

Loomis could feel a knot starting to form in her stomach.

"Gee, do I dare to ask? she answered.

"Actually," Delaney started, "I think that bad news is the wrong choice of words. I should have said that I have some very strange information to share with you and your team." Delaney paused.

Still feeling a little nauseous Nancy waited for him to explain.

"Our agents tracked both Silva and Dr. Harding back to the hotel where they normally stayed across from the chapel. The Banshees meanwhile sailed with Fielding but got off the yacht and transferred to ATVs. We lost them in the bush but knew that they would eventually set up camp somewhere near the chapel." He paused.

"Well, so far it sounds like everything was going as planned. What happened?" Loomis asked.

No answer for a long time and just before Loomis called out to see if Delaney was still there, he came back on line saying, "We don't know what happened. There was a tremendous storm overhead with lightning strikes touching down. My two agents took cover but could still see Silva and later Dr. Harding approach the chapel and then nothing."

"What do you mean nothing?" asked Loomis. "Nothing happened. They saw Silva for a moment in the downpour but it was as if he just disappeared. Dr. Harding made it inside he chapel, but never came out. It was not safe to check the exterior of the back of the chapel until daybreak and at that time, my agents climbing through the brush, found ATVs but no one could be seen or heard. They used their binoculars and looked at the rear of the chapel, but did not see any sign of entry. Soon they heard a bell ring and quickly retraced their steps to observed the front door of the building.

Out came the guardian who walked up the front gate. He picked up what appeared to be a bag of groceries and placed in near the front door. He then took a walk around the entire exterior of the building and then picked up the groceries and enter the chapel, closing the door behind him."

"Where was Dr. Harding?" Loomis asked.

"Both she and Silva simply disappeared. I have no other information as to where they went or where their current location is – and there is more. The yacht is missing. I had the Federal Police send out a patrol boat to locate the vessel, thinking that perhaps, somehow, they had a plan B that we were not aware of, but we came up empty handed. I used some agencies around the region to see if they had a radar fix on the vessel. One location stated that they saw a blimp for a few minutes, but then it went off the screen."

"Jesus, you mean that not only have we lost contact with everyone involved but even the God-damn yacht? What the fuck do we do now? Sorry, pardon my French," Loomis said.

There was a noticeable silence on the line until Delaney broke it by saying that he felt all the two agencies can do is wait and see again. If anyone raised their heads, whether it be Silva, Dr. Harding, any of the Banshees or the yacht, then then could pick up the investigation, but until then, they had to concentrate on the follow-up investigation regarding the stash hidden in a cave in Afghanistan.

Chapter 60

The same morning, hearing the same news report on his radio, the guardian, closed the Bible that he was reading and lite some incense near the Ark. He turned off the broadcast, made up his bunk and decided to take a walk in the courtyard. He was greeted at the main gate by a single pilgrim who was in the process of placing a bag of groceries near the entrance. The guardian thanked and blessed the individual and began walking back to the entrance of the chapel. He stopped before entering and placed the bag to the right of the door. He then started to walk slowly down the side of the chapel nearest the main church. He then turned left walking the perimeter of the back to the chapel. The ground was moist from the night's rain but he had no problem with his footing.

He glanced at the foliage on the other side of the iron gate and commented to himself what a beautiful day it will be today. Making another left turn, he walked the last side of the chapel ending up at its entrance. He reached down and picked up the bag and returned to the interior of the building.

He placed the groceries in the refrigerator and made himself a cup of tea. He turned the radio back on but changed the channel to a religious music station playing chants. He grabbed his bible and laid back down on his cot.

In the next room, behind the gold inlay wooden door, the Ark stood majestically on the altar, the sunlight glistening on its lid.

www.ingramcontent.com/pod-product-compliance
Lightning Source LLC
Chambersburg PA
CBHW060552310726
48982CB00008B/1094/J

9780998877730